Dakhma

Dakhma

K Hari Kumar

HarperCollins *Publishers* India

First published in India by
HarperCollins *Publishers* 2021
A-75, Sector 57, Noida, Uttar Pradesh 201301, India
www.harpercollins.co.in

2 4 6 8 10 9 7 5 3 1

P-ISBN: 978-93-5489-062-8
E-ISBN: 978-93-5489-278-3

Cover design and illustration by Nitesh Mohanty.

Typeset in 11/14 Adobe Caslon Pro at
Manipal Technologies Limited, Manipal

Printed and bound at
Thomson Press (India) Ltd

HarperCollinsIn

to my mother.

'The oldest and strongest emotion of mankind is fear, and the oldest and strongest kind of fear is the fear of the unknown.'
—H.P. Lovecraft

Part I

The Woman at the
Glass Door

Prologue

17 July 1999, Saturday
7E, Paradise Heights, Mumbai

*D*EATH — *IT INSTILS IN ONE A FEELING THAT WHATEVER happens ... just happens. Different people have different theories, and for ages, humankind could not decipher its mysterious nature, neither through the spectres of religion nor through the spectacles of science.*

Death — it confirms that at the end of the day, this life has just one purpose, an inevitable end. All those curiosities of infanthood, obsessions of adolescence, and ambitions of adulthood just spiral back into a womb of nothingness. Death.

Death — it negates the existence of infinity and the absence of the Infinite. All the tenets that become the basis of religion and philosophy simply vanish, and the claim of knowledge of the unknown validates uncertainty of the highest degree.

The mind fears the unknown, and it becomes jittery when it has to ponder about death. People fear death, and what happens after that, or perhaps what happens to the person at that precise moment ...

The lights went off inside apartment 7E. Flashes of lightning disturbed the dark room through the balcony's glass door. Parizaad stopped writing. She raised the tip of her fountain pen from the coarse page of the diary. Amidst the rumbling of thunder, she could swear she heard the faint creak of the front door.

Is it here, already? Parizaad wondered. *No, not tonight.*

But there it was again – the creaking.

It is here! The scavenger is here for me. She was sure she had heard this sound before – just not in that house. With trembling hands, she picked up the pen's cap from the desk and screwed it back on. From the top drawer, she grabbed her lighter and rolled the metal spark down with a trembling thumb, until flame erupted, bringing into focus a posh teakwood bed, the writing desk, the chair, the dressing table, and some vintage lampshades in the room. In the dim warm light of the single flame, everything seemed to glow a faint yellow, including Parizaad's pale skin and her frilly maroon gown.

She rose from the wooden chair. *Why is it coming from the living room?* In Parizaad's experience, the feeling of this unknown entity approaching her had always come from the balcony, through the glass door. Tonight, it was coming from the front room.

Her legs wobbled as she made her way towards the door. She put out the flame, and it was dark again. Outside, the storm raged on. Once at the front door, she bent and peeped through the keyhole. A flash of lightning illuminated everything, and in that brief moment, she saw something swish in front of the door. Parizaad recoiled in fear. Was it a shadow or the apparition of the *scavenger*?

She gathered herself and bolted the door from inside. She took a few steps back, ignited the lighter again, and walked towards the bed. Her seven-year-old daughter was sleeping, ignorant of everything that her mother had been fighting. *My little angel*, Parizaad thought, and quickly pattered towards her. *How do I protect you from this monster? There is no place we can run.* She wished she had never come back from Delhi. Her daughter would have been safer in the capital city. Her eyes welled up and a tear fell on the left cheek of the little girl, waking her up.

'Mom?' The girl touched her cheek where it was still wet from the tear. 'Why are you crying, Mom?'

Parizaad gathered all the courage that she could. 'Promise me you will be a brave girl tonight?'

The girl nodded.

'Then come with me.'

The girl got up from the bed and held her mother's right hand, and they walked towards the balcony. They were seven floors above the ground, and the skies seemed nearer from there. Thunder gurgled, sending bolts of lightning into the night sky. Clouds had darkened, gathered in numbers. The strange presence that had consumed Parizaad's mind had now manifested in the skies. The little girl could only see the clouds, but Parizaad saw what hovered around them in circles.

'Please save us from this devil, oh God!' the woman cried, looking towards the sky. 'At least save my daughter. Please do not punish her for the sin that she never committed. I beg you, God! I just need to survive this night, so that I can tell the truth to the world in the morning.'

Drops of rain poured from the sky.

Just one more night, Oh God! Are you even alive?

Meanwhile, the scavenger had entered the bedroom. It had access to every room in that apartment in Paradise Heights. The darkness inside the room did not deter it; it could still see clearly. It tore off the freshly written page from Parizaad's diary, crumpled it, and put it inside its pocket. The world would never know what happened, and who did it if the sole evidence was destroyed. The scavenger knew she was outside; afraid and helpless. It glided towards the glass door that led to the balcony. Parizaad could see the diabolic presence coming towards her, and before she could blink, it was at the glass door, turning the knob, sliding it open. As it stood there, the woman saw the scavenger staring right into her soul. She tightened her grip around her daughter's wrist and dragged her behind her back in an attempt to hide her from the monster. There was little else she could do at this point. Holding on to her daughter's hand, Parizaad was losing hope, knowing she would not be able to protect her daughter. The scavenger tilted its head diabolically. At that moment Parizaad recollected what she had written in her diary, moments ago:

The mind fears the unknown, and it becomes jittery when it has to ponder about death. People fear death, and what happens after that, or perhaps they fear what happens to the person at the precise moment that death arrives …

That moment was now.

1

31 July 2019, Wednesday
Sohna Road, Gurugram

'TINSEL IS CELEBRATING TODAY BECAUSE OF THE TEAM'S efforts led by the master strategist Varun Anand!' declared Ashwath Desai, the seed investor of the Gurugram based start-up. The twenty attendees in the conference room cheered. The cheerful applause sounded like raindrops falling on an asbestos roof. Desai, a plump man in his early sixties, wore his signature blue trousers and tuxedo. He smiled at the young man who was sitting in the front row. 'Varun, the stage is all yours, beta.'

The audience, which comprised the team leads, creative artists, content writers, marketing executives, and telecom operators, broke into a louder applause. Varun stood up, revealing his lean six-foot-two-inch frame, and walked towards the centre of the conference room. The light-brown stubble on his chiselled face was a head-turner for quite a few women in the little organization that had suddenly grown by leaps and bounds. Desai welcomed his star with an embrace.

'Thank you, Mr Desai. Thanks for giving *us* this opportunity and don't forget to thank yourself for pumping the monies!' Varun said, showing no signs of modesty. After all, a few months ago Tinsel was just an idea in Varun's brain until the Mumbai-based Desai poured a few crores into it.

Desai smiled. He walked to his chair, the biggest one in the room, and sat down. Despite being one of the biggest angel investors in the country, he never patronized his finds, which earned him a lot of respect from the young employees.

When the cheer died down a bit, Varun continued, 'The past six months have been exhausting. But before that, we didn't even exist. Thanks to our efforts … right from Jaggi guarding our gates to the lovely Ms Jasleen juggling my schedule.' He shot a glance at his dusky middle-aged secretary, noticing the blush on her heart-shaped face. 'The victory of our client, People's Party of Delhi, has proved that we can achieve anything if we put our blood and sweat into it.' Varun spoke with pride of their first client. 'We baptized the party from an old repellent name. We chose the right strategy for its almost never-before-known candidates; we were at it during every step. Today, our client is ruling the Delhi assembly. This is what we do; we use new media and data science to influence our voters.' He shot a glance at the fresh interns. A lot of nodding heads in the group. Varun moved his face closer to the microphone. 'Forty-eight out of seventy seats. Nobody expected that from a party that was contesting elections for the first time. Our strong social media strategies restricted our client's rival, a national party, to a mere nineteen seats.' Varun waited for the words to sink-in.

'Tinsel does not stand by the principles of the party. But it stands by the client, it always will, regardless of their ideology. We are at the helm of a social-media revolution. We leverage news in a way that helps our client. We plant opinions in the minds of the voter. We are the *kingmakers* of this digital era.' Varun looked at the surrounding employees, took a deep breath and asked, 'Did you think that the last six months were exhausting? Did you have sleepless nights? No, it wasn't exhausting. It was a *cakewalk*.'

His words surprised a few, but most of the folks in the room knew what their boss was going to say. 'Now, we have another biggie coming up. Maharashtra! If we can win in Delhi with a new party, imagine where we can reach with an already established party. Get ready for more remote networking and overtime! Don't feel ashamed to ask for incentives, guys! Not even a pandemic should be able to stop us …'

More applause. Varun smiled. Ashwath got up from his chair and kept his warm hand on Varun's back as they walked out of the conference room.

⁓

'Tinsel is now the most sought-after political campaign management agency in the country. You know, beta, I was doubtful when you came to me with this idea of an image consultancy for political parties. I mean, in a country like ours, I never expected Tinsel to grow at this speed in such a brief span.' Desai opened the packet of Marlboro and offered it to Varun.

Varun pulled out one cigarette from the pack of twenty. Looking at the rolled white tobacco product he said, 'So far, international agencies looked after the political image and PR of the national parties. But these days everyone is a politician on Twitter, taking sides and waging virtual wars. So, an indigenous political PR agency that was affordable to smaller players had to find takers. Everybody is improving their image using PR agencies – indie filmmakers, social media influencers, garage start-ups, and even book writers!'

Desai chuckled at the last one. He said, 'Yeah, I know an ex-government employee who pumped his life's savings into marketing a self-published book a few years back. Now he is one of the biggest writers in the country. He is a total rage at lit fests!'

'Ethics contradict the art of selling, Mr Desai.' Varun was unapologetic. 'We are working at one-tenth the price that international image consultants charge. As long as we can, let us capitalize on the trend. Few years down the line, every college dropout will start their own election campaign management and PR agency.'

'There will be a political party mushrooming from every garage, is what I hear.' Desai lit another cigarette with his Japanese lighter, which had a shiny golden chain winding around a plated spherical body. 'Light?' he offered Varun, noticing that he was still holding the cigarette.

'No, thank you. I quit smoking.'

'Well, why did you take one out of my box?'

'I like to hold this in my hand. See how long I can hold on to the urge. Did you know that the companies that manufacture branded cigarettes add glycerol, cocoa and even sugars to enhance its, how do you say … taste?'

Desai shrugged. 'I just like to smoke them; don't feel the taste anymore.'

'Little things that can kill you.' Varun's eyes lingered on the statutory graphic displayed on the pack lying on the desk. The disturbing image of the damaged lungs made his heart sink a bit. Then he though, *Not a great way to market it, but people still don't quit. A perfect example of the boomerang effect.*

'Anyway, Varun,' Desai said in his guttural voice, circling back to business, 'I have news for you.'

Varun looked at the older business person.

'I spoke with someone from MNP today. They told me that MNP will offer three times more than what the People's Party is offering for the upcoming elections in Maharashtra.'

'Excellent!' Varun almost jumped with excitement. 'I told you they will take the bait.'

'I thought you would go with the People's Party of Maharashtra since you already have a working relationship with them in Delhi.' Desai's face betrayed his discomfort with the situation..

'Mr Desai, I told you … ethics …'

' … contradict the art of selling,' Desai completed. 'Yeah, yeah, I know how you think, beta.'

'I know you do not approve of my style of business. You are old school. Let our prospective clients know we are here for the big monies. This is business. Let us not talk about loyalty. The People's Party did not do us any favour. We made them what they are today. If they want us in Maharashtra, let them estimate our value correctly.' Varun placed his unlit cigarette back inside the pack. 'Otherwise, they can go back to where they came from.'

'Beta, I have been doing business for over forty years now. I started when I was fourteen, selling tea to customers outside Rivoli on rainy evenings. This is what I have learned …' he paused for effect, ' … sometimes you might owe things that come back to haunt you when you least expect it.'

'And that is why I will owe nothing to anyone. We do things for those who pay us well. Simple!' Varun stated.

'But you just said you wanted to work at one-tenth the price.'

'Yes, I did. And we will if the client is independent. But when it is a big fish like the Maharashtra Nationalist Party, you don't think small.'

Desai sighed. 'When I call you beta, you know I mean it. Right?'

'Yes.'

'Good. That is why I am asking you to reconsider the offer from People's Party. I know MNP very well. They are bullies, and once you get entangled with them, there is no getting out until Bhau lets you,' Desai warned. 'It will not be a cakewalk.'

'Yes, and you've got to trust me, one more time,' Varun requested. 'I am sure I am going to sign a contract with MNP. There are no second thoughts in my mind now.'

'Tinsel is your baby. I am just putting in money until it can stand on its own feet.'

Varun acknowledged Desai's statement with a smile.

Desai took another drag on his cigarette. 'How is your wife doing?'

'She is stable now.'

'You haven't been around for her, son. I think you should spend some time with her before you start with the next client.'

'How much time do we have?' Varun pulled out his phone, opened his schedule and checked. 'Hardly a week, I guess. But I should head to Mumbai by Monday.'

'Why don't you and your wife spend a week at the Taj? My gift to you for all the work that you have done here. You deserve it.'

'Please, Mr Desai. I can't accept that.'

'Oh, come on, beta! This is the least I can do for you. I know you well enough to assume that you don't wish to waste any time to connect with your next client. You can use the stay to connect with Bhau.'

The idea made sense to Varun. He had already started calculating how much time he could save by utilizing the weekend to set up an ad hoc base in Mumbai.

Desai exhaled smoke into the air and said, 'Now why don't you go home, pack everything you need and wait for your cab? I am sure your wife would love the grand view of the sea from the Taj. That is until you find an apartment to suit your need.'

'No time for a retreat, Mr Desai. Tinsel has an election to win for my client.'

'Sure, sure. By the way, I would love to meet your wife once you are in Mumbai. It is long overdue.'

A look of worry clouded Varun's face. 'Well, actually, she is still trying to cope with her anxieties. Anahita does not attend parties or gatherings with me, and eventually all the time she spends alone aggravates her social anxiety even more.'

'Well, whenever it has to happen, it will. Let destiny take its course. But you really need to give her more time, beta. A lot more time.' He extended his hand to Varun.

Varun shook hands with his boss and smiled. 'Of course. See you in Mumbai.'

'See you there, son.' As Desai watched the ambitious young man leave the room, he was reminded of how he used to be thirty years ago. He had high hopes for Varun.

2

'Anahita, are you sure you want to proceed with this?' Dr Malhotra spoke, boring her ageing grey eyes into the twinkling brown ones of the pale young woman sitting on the couch on the other side of the doctor's desk.

The young client, Anahita Anand, nodded. Her red-coloured strappy midi dress was tailormade to suit her svelte frame.

The questioning look in the doctor's eyes magnified on the lens of her carbon-rimmed eyeglasses. 'And you don't want to tell your husband about this?'

'I am afraid that he will not understand. Not at this moment, he wouldn't.'

'But in two months, your bump will start showing. What will you do then?'

The idea terrified Anahita, and she shifted uncomfortably in her seat. She stammered, 'I'll … I … w-will find a way.' She decided against explaining herself further. *Anxiety.* After all, this woman wasn't her mother – just a professional she was paying to listen to her.

'Anahita, you have been seeing me since you were a teenager. I know you very well. You are capable of burying things without letting anyone find out. But this is not a *past* secret ... this is ... well ... your future. And both of you are involved in it – Varun and you.' The doctor sighed. 'I am advising against this. He should know that you are carrying his baby.'

His *baby? Is it not mine? It is* our *baby, for God's sake!* Anahita pricked the leather skin of her handbag with her fingernails.

'I know you do that when you feel unbearable stress,' Dr Malhotra said, observing Anahita's involuntary action. 'You want to give up, but your mind doesn't let you.'

Anahita stopped her compulsive fidgeting and sighed. 'Varun has been against having a child. He needs time, he says. I am sure this happened that night when both of us were drunk. There was no other way I could have ...' Anahita stopped herself. Even though her therapist knew, Anahita did not want to acknowledge her inability to make love with her husband while sober. 'You know very well what I have been going through. I am so stupid!'

'Repulsed ... not *stupid*. But you can't be with that fear forever. We have been working on multiple phobias. We have made progress with a few. I mean, until four years ago, you couldn't walk on the road by yourself. Now you can! You are no more disturbed by visual or auditory hallucinations. You have recovered well but everything has taken time, effort and the support of your family. This will too.'

'I feel I am running out of time. As for support, I want to have a baby, he doesn't want it at this stage of his career.'

'What about *your* career?'

'I don't have one. I have done nothing in a decade. I can't be around strangers without someone accompanying me.'

'But you can try meeting new people through Varun.'

Anahita smiled half-heartedly. 'I am sure that he does not want me in his professional world. I am just a nuisance.'

'Well, let go of these thoughts of low self-worth. You are a wonderful human being, full of potential. Regarding the baby …' She paused, removed her glasses and continued, 'as your psychiatrist, I told you what I thought was best. You should inform him.'

'I will … when the time is right,' Anahita said, this time with a mild glow of confidence on her face. She smiled and got up from the couch.

'All right, Anahita. Call me anytime. Given your history, you may get cramps and fake menstrual symptoms. You will get panic attacks for sure. You can continue with the regular prescription. Although you haven't had visual hallucinations in a long time, take Cypene-10 only in case you have one. And please consult a gynae at the earliest.'

'Yes, Dr Malhotra. I will. Goodbye!'

As Anahita walked towards the door, she felt relieved. She had been seeing her psychiatrist every month since the monsoon of 2008. Dr Malhotra knew more about Anahita than Anahita herself. As she exited the room, the doctor pressed on the buzzer and spoke into it, 'Send the next one in, will you?'

3

❦

South City 2, Gurugram

It drizzled at noon. July always brought that much-awaited spell of rain, which turned the dry city into a tropical paradise. The petrichor mated with the pungent fumes of the exhaust pipes of vehicles that congested the busy roads of the Millennium City. Gurugram had grown from a mere patch of neglected township to one of the most sought-after modern cities in South Asia. It now boasted the highest human development index in the Indian subcontinent. Yet, the stretch of road that connected Sohna Road with the posh residential complex was now brimming with stagnant rainwater on one side – the perk of living in a modern Indian city. The other side of the road was wet from the rain, as was the pavement. Anahita held a black umbrella in her right hand as she walked, its steel tube below the polyvinyl runner resting above her shoulder. Occasionally, a drop of water or two would trickle from the tip of the umbrella on to the red fabric of her dress.

In her mind, insecurities swirled. She wondered if she had done the right thing by revealing the pregnancy to Dr Malhotra. *What if she passed the secret to Varun?* As Anahita walked past a couple of food joints, she realized she was the only one on the pavement. The incident from her adolescence troubled Anahita to that day. The acute stress disorder triggered anxiety and multiple phobias, and one of those ruined her marriage with Varun Anand. She always wanted to have a baby, but the very thought of sexual contact gave her chills. She found a solution after three years of matrimony but it came at a heavy price – her sanity.

Maybe I should stop seeing Dr Malhotra. I needed her support in the past because of whatever happened. I don't get those dreams anymore, yet I feel like I am living in the shadows of what happened fourteen years ago. I need to move on … but I need her support to move on.

As contradicting thoughts filled her fragile mind, Anahita saw a shadow pass over her peripheral vision. She stopped in her tracks and turned around, but there was no sign of anyone.

I must've imagined that. I won't give in; I can do this. I won't let my anxiety control me. Bracing herself, Anahita resumed walking, and before long, she saw the large entrance gate of her gated society at a distance. There was a smaller pedestrian gate next to the large one. As she reached it, she was struck by the same feeling again – as though someone was behind her. This time, she did not turn around, and entered the gate. As she passed by the guard's cabin and walked towards the second block – where her apartment building was – the old man with damaged teeth and balding head greeted her with a salaam. Anahita responded with a sweet smile and carried on.

Seconds later, she felt a presence behind her – *again*. She was standing in front of the elevator now, and something brushed by her hair. Anahita turned around with a jerk. 'Who's there?' Not a single soul anywhere, except the lanky watchman who stood two hundred metres away. Something didn't feel right. The poor old chap smiled again. She looked through him as if he did not exist. Pearls of sweat gathered on her forehead.

Dr Malhotra was right. I still need her support.

She looked at the elevator; the doors were open. *Wasn't this closed? When did I press the button?* Confusion. She remembered what an old friend had suggested to overcome one of those anxious moments; *close your eyes tightly … breathe in … breathe out.* Anahita entered the elevator, pressed the button to close it and then the one that read '3'. The metallic doors of the elevator closed, and the contraption moved upwards.

Until 2015, Anahita feared those shiny elevator doors. It was so bad that she could not step inside an elevator, even if someone was with her. It took her a while, but now she could travel in the elevator to her apartment by herself. *I guess I owe it to Dr Malhotra's efforts.* Anahita reminded herself. However, she was sure that she could not step inside any other elevator until she was familiar with it; she was claustrophobic, and the fear aggravated in unfamiliar places. She sometimes wondered if she had all the phobias that a human mind could accommodate. Her psychiatrist had once told her that a part of her brain was damaged, a small part called the amygdala.

As the elevator stopped at her floor and the doors opened, Anahita opened her eyes and sighed in relief. She stepped out into the broad corridor; there were six houses on that floor, three on her left and three on her right. She walked towards the first one on the right. She pressed her finger on the scanner at the door and made her way in. The smart light inside the living room sensed the mistress, and it turned on. She felt safe. She closed the door behind her and went straight to the bathroom to freshen up. The day was too humid.

⁓

Twenty minutes later, Anahita was in the kitchen preparing a cup of coffee for herself. She called on Varun's phone, but he did not answer. *Busy, as usual.* That is how it had been for the last six months, ever since he resigned from his previous job and floated his start-up. *Tinsel* – Anahita had suggested that name, and that was the only time he had taken her suggestion on anything in the recent past. The people in his workplace called him the brain behind the organization. Not that she ever complained about it. While Varun scaled the commercial ladder, Anahita's life passed by like a routine. On occasions, Vatsala, her mother came over. Anahita did not like the dictatorial ways of her mother, but she knew that was the mother's way of loving an emotionally unstable daughter. *No thoughts of low self-worth!* Anahita reminded herself.

Three weeks ago, Anahita had felt her first bout of morning sickness. At first, she thought it was food poisoning. She had missed her periods too. Her physician suggested taking a pregnancy test. She still remembered purchasing that packet of home pregnancy kit first thing in the morning and peeing on its back in the confines of her bathroom. As the little drops of urine trickled over the patch, the silica granules absorbed enough moisture to throw up two pink bands – it was positive. She was pregnant! She held the stick in her right hand and stared at it, confused by what this news meant for her married life and her husband's career. Will he accept their baby?

Now, as she started at the mug of coffee in her hand, she was sitting on the couch in the living room, recalling the moment she first discovered her pregnancy, Anahita thought, *I think he deserves to know. If he really loves me, he will accept my decision.*

The doorbell rang, disrupting her thoughts. She placed the mug on the side table as the door opened to Varun's touch. Anahita ran to him and held him in an embrace. She practised the sentence in her mind: *I have a surprise for you, my love!*

'I have a surprise for you!' Varun said, taking Anahita's words right out of her mouth.

I was going to say that. Anahita stared at her husband without blinking her eyes, surprised.

Varun tossed his black leather bag on to the couch on which Anahita was sitting a few seconds ago, missing the mug on the table by a few inches. He lifted his wife in his arms and kissed her. 'We are going to Mumbai!'

'Wow, that is a surprise.'

'Well, I have been expecting it for some time now, truth be told,' Varun revealed. 'Now you can pursue full-time modelling as well, if you wish! You could even pursue acting! I remember you had told me you wanted become an actor once.'

Anahita had mentioned her unfulfilled dream on their first date. She could not forget that. 'Oh, Varun! That was, like, long ago. I don't have such ambitions now.'

'This is huge!' He exclaimed dismissing Anahita's response altogether. 'I had been working the folks at Mumbai to give us the bigger deal, and they did!'

'I am so happy for you!'

The floor felt suddenly colder. Anahita really wanted to tell him about the baby. Her mind was racing. She was conscious of her breathing – fast and shallow. *Come on, Anahita, tell him you are expecting a baby. He is happy for himself, but he has to be happy for you too.* But she only managed to say, 'Can I make you something? Coffee?'

Varun spotted the mug of hot coffee. He picked it up and sipped from it. 'This will do. I hope you are happy too.'

'Yes,' she lied. *I will not be happy until you hear my surprise. I am pregnant with our child.*

'And Mr Desai has given us a week's time to stay in the Taj. Grand suite with a seaside view!'

'Wow! Mr Desai does like you a lot.'

'Yeah, he is like the father I never had. But I am making him a huge chunk of money as well. The poor old chap is too much into ethics and all. He just doesn't get it. I wonder how he survived all these years.'

'Haha, you can *try* to be modest, Varun.' Anahita smiled through pursed lips.

'Yeah, okay. I'll try. You should start packing, by the way. We are leaving early morning. We have the weekend to ourselves; after that, we need to find a good place to move in. I will leave that up to you. I'll be busy meeting the biggest folks from Indian politics and the industrial sector. Literally, the people who run the country!'

Anahita had stopped listening to Varun. She could only focus on the voice in her head: *Tell him about the baby or I am going to faint.* Pearls of sweat trickle down her pretty face.

'I'm going to have a warm bath in the tub.' Varun removed his blazer and sauntered towards their bedroom. 'You can join me.'

You are a coward, Anahita. Coward! Her mind gave up.

'I am coming, dear.'

As Anahita walked to the bathroom, the smart light turned off on its own. The living room plunged into darkness, as it had been before.

4

1 August 2019, Thursday
Mumbai

THE DRIZZLE KEPT THE AIR AND THE ASPHALT MOIST. Anahita and Varun got into a private Innova after landing at the domestic terminal of Chhatrapati Shivaji Maharaj International Airport. The man who received them at arrival had introduced himself as Keshav Mhatre. He was short and stout, with an evil-looking scar above his left eye. Anahita felt uncomfortable looking at his eye. It reminded her of Christopher, her classmate from middle school. She was afraid of the boy until she was eighteen. But Keshav seemed like a nice guy, and her husband did not seem to mind the scar. In fact, Varun was perhaps too occupied to even notice; he was going through some emails on his iPhone. He asked the driver to turn off the music so he could work in peace and rolled up the windows to shut out the noise of the traffic. The smell of air freshener circulating in the closed off car gave Anahita a headache. She closed her eyes, bored with the streets and signals on the Western Express Highway. It was just blackness, accompanied by the subtle sound of the SUV's air conditioner and occasional honking of vehicles outside.

I am going to start a new chapter in my life. I'm going to fall in love with you again, Mumbai! Visuals of shooting floors and studios from 2010 flashed before her eyes. About nine years ago, a casting agency had called her up for an ad shoot in Mumbai. Anahita had just turned eighteen, and that was the first time she had set foot in *the city of dreams*, as they called it. She felt a sense of familiarity in the city; an unflinching perception of belonging to something that she had never felt before in her life. After that, they called her a dozen times within a year and her casting coordinator advised Anahita to move, as that would make her more accessible for assignments. The casting coordinator, Mehr, was her former classmate until sixth grade, and had once been Anahita's best friend. While working together, they became very close once again. Mehr predicted a sparkling career in showbiz for Anahita, but her mother would never allow her to move to Mumbai. Anahita blamed herself for that. She had always been a coward.

The screeching sound of the cab interrupted Anahita's trip down memory lane. Her stream of thought came crashing as she opened her eyes to the sound of traffic outside.

'*Aaijavadya,*' Keshav cussed out of the window that was now pulled down. Inches away from the bonnet stood a bewildered little boy of about six. He wore a tattered grey kurta. Keshav spat at the boy's feet. '*Dusaryacya gadikhali ka marata nahi? Hatt lawdeya!*'

'*Chalo chalo!*' Varun told the driver to move on.

The driver rolled up the window, abruptly cutting off the cacophony outside. As the car slowly started moving, the boy outside took a few steps back. Anahita saw fear in his eyes.

'Sir, once Bhau comes to power, he will send these immigrants back to where they came from.' The driver looked at Varun's reflection in the rear-view mirror.

Varun hummed, his attention now back on his phone. 'Anahita,' he spoke without looking away from the screen.

'Yeah?'

'I have a few meetings tomorrow and the day after. I hope you won't mind.'

Anahita looked at him but did not speak.

'Is it okay if I don't join you for the apartment hunt? I am sure Keshav will take you around?'

'Of course, sir. I will take her wherever she wants to go. Don't worry. Just tell me which locality you want to see. I know of all the places in South Mumbai,' Keshav replied.

'Anahita?' Varun smiled at his wife. 'I want you to find a house where you would want to live. I'll be at work most of the time, you know.'

She knew he was saying that because he did not want to be bothered with a house hunt. He had work to do. It hurt her, but she pretended as if it did not. 'Sure, I will look around.'

'Great!' Varun exclaimed. He put his left arm around Anahita's shoulder and pulled her towards his chest. She rested her head on him. There was still a heart that was beating under the shiny suit. 'I love you,' she said.

'I love you too, darling.'

Anahita closed her eyes once again. Blackness took over, but this time there was the warm sound of her spouse's heartbeat to keep her company. She wondered if there was any room left for her anymore.

5

2 August 2019, Friday
MNP Headquarters

THE RECENTLY CONSTRUCTED GRAND BUILDING overlooked one of the busiest junctions in the southern part of the city. From outside, it looked like a modern mall with non-reflective glass dominating the exterior made of rosewood. From inside the building, one could see the world outside. Varun sat on a white sofa in the lounge area next to the reception – legs crossed, reading the day's newspaper. A table made of thick glass stood at a distance from where he sat. The interior walls were white too; white was MNP's colour – it represented *purity*, according to its founder, Dayanand Deshmukh.

The receptionist was a short woman with a heart-shaped face and thick carbon-rimmed glasses, her white polyester shirt buttoned up to the neck. She had introduced herself as Rekha. The telephone on the desk had a receiver carved of ivory, just like all the little decorative items in the building.

When Dayanand Deshmukh, or Bhau as everyone called him, inaugurated the office a few months ago, he had expected the media to go gaga over the luxurious feel of the party's new abode. However, his expectations dimmed out when one of the regional media channels aired a debate over the use of ivory. The news saw animal rights activists protesting and filing a case against Bhau, but inspection concluded that the material used for making the furniture was a synthetic polymer – faux ivory. This brought a lot of bad press for the channel, and the loyal supporters of the party hurled stones outside the news channel's headquarters in Bandra. Later, the party supporters intercepted the channel founder's car at his apartment's parking area. This became a talking point on national news, and Bhau stepped in, asking his supporters to forgive the channel for its 'foolishness'. Bhau became the all-forgiving hero – even for those who had earlier opposed him. Since the incident, the regional channel stopped airing any news that went against the party. Varun was aware of the influence that Bhau had over a certain section of the society, but that was not enough for the man to win a state election. He needed a makeover; he needed the support of the working class and the business owners. Varun was here to bring that change.

'Mr Varun Anand?'

Varun looked up. Rekha had walked over from her desk.

'Bhau will see you now,' she said, her voice mechanical.

'Thanks.' Varun folded the paper and placed it back on the glass table. He rose from his sofa and adjusted his coat.

'Come with me, Mr Anand.'

'Please. Call me Varun.'

Rekha's thick red lips caught his eye, reminding him of his personal assistant from Gurugram. As his eyes lingered, the left corner of her lips curled up, pushing the cheek on that side – a seductive smile. She turned and started walking towards a room at a hundred meters. As he followed her, Varun ran his eyes from the back of her head to her hip, which curved like a pistol right above the pear-shaped bottom. The black trousers shielded her beauty from his imagination.

They arrived at the room. Rekha stopped, pulled the latch, and opened the door for Varun to go inside. He could see a broad-shouldered man sitting on the chair, going through some papers, signing them. He had seen Bhau on the television and in newspapers for more than a decade, but this was the first time he was seeing the grand politician in person. Varun walked in and Rekha closed the door behind him.

'Mr Anand!' Bhau kept the papers away and welcomed Varun. The politician removed his glasses and placed them folded over the stack of papers. There was a stainless-steel flask and a couple of inverted tumblers nearby. He gestured towards the empty chair across from him.

'It is an honour to meet you, Mr Deshmukh,' Varun spoke in a formal tone while taking the chair. He realized that Bhau's face looked broader than it did in media photos and videos. His nose had this peculiar plumpness, a feature that cartoonists used to exploit in their caricatures. He looked about sixty, maybe a little more, and his dressing style was simple.

'I have heard a lot about you from my sources. They say that you single-handedly managed PPD's victory. Is that so?' The big man picked up a tumbler and started pouring tea from the flask.

'Depends on who you mean by *they*.'

'Tea?'

'Yes, please.'

Bhau pushed the tumbler towards Varun, who picked it up, blew into the hot milk tea and took a sip.

Bhau observed him for a while before speaking. 'In 2015, our party allied with a national party and our coalition swept the state assembly election. But as you know, our allies stabbed us in the back when they ran independently in the Lok Sabha polls. Of course, there were other issues as well that I don't care about. I want the best for my people, my state. Those national parties do not understand the pulse of the local people like I do. Maharashtra is looking for a young Marathi leader, someone educated in English but who can speak its people's mother tongue. A charismatic persona that can attract the youth, which makes up 25 per cent of the voters. Trust me, Mr Anand, these youngsters do not identify themselves with a caste or gotra. They have outgrown the caste-based politics that dominated until last decade.' Bhau paused to pour tea in his tumbler. A moment later, he continued, 'When I talk to them, I do not see pride for their land or mother tongue in their eyes. I see a thirst for better living standards and higher payouts. For them, I am just an ageing politician of a bygone era.' Bhau sipped tea from his tumbler.

Varun hesitated; the first sip had been too sweet for his taste. But Bhau gave him no choice. Varun knew how to adjust to a client's requirements; he gulped down some more of the sugary concoction and put the tumbler down. 'We can change that outlook, Mr Deshmukh. We—'

'No, you do not have to do that,' Bhau interrupted.

'Then?'

A moment's silence.

'I want you to project my nephew, Abhinav, as their leader – as the face of the youth. That is why I roped in the best in the business' – the old politician peered at Varun – 'at the best price you can ever imagine.'

'But Mr Deshmukh,' Varun chose his words carefully, 'the election is six months away and you have never projected Abhinav as a political leader before.' Varun shifted in his chair with unease.

'That is why I hired you. You must understand Mr Anand,' Bhau said, leaning forward, 'I dislike giving options to my people. They are either with me or … ' The old politician let his words trail off and raised the tumbler of tea. 'I hope you liked the tea.'

Varun knew what that meant. There was never a choice. He had to drink the tea offered to him. Bhau had made it very clear. Varun took a last sip and placed the empty tumbler on the table. 'I need to meet Abhinav at the earliest.'

'I will arrange the meeting. Why don't you come over to my mother's birthday celebration at my place? She is turning eighty this Friday. I will introduce you to my nephew, and the two of you can talk in my study.'

'Sounds good to me.'

'By that time, you can settle down as well. I hope that my boy, Keshav, is doing a decent job. Did he show you the properties in Malabar Hill?'

'I am not getting involved with that. As it is, I will hardly be home. My wife has gone with him. But yeah, Keshav told me he has a few properties to show her.'

'Well, those are some of the nicest properties I own in the city. I don't normally give them out; they are reserved for special guests. So the rent is on me.' Bhau winked at Varun.

'Of course, Mr Deshmukh.' Varun rose from his chair and shook hands with Bhau. 'Have a nice day.'

6

2 August 2019, Friday

BY THE TIME ANAHITA WOKE UP, HER HUSBAND HAD already left for the day. He had scribbled a note for her, now kept on the bedside table. She rubbed her eyes and picked up the yellow sticky note: *Don't wait for me, will be late. Keshav will take you around. He has a list of houses.*

'This is so typical of you, Varun.' Anahita got up from the bed and headed to the bathroom, dropping the note in the waste bin on her way.

An hour later, Anahita was sitting inside the Innova. Keshav wore a sky-blue kurta over black pyjamas.

'Keshav?'

'Yes, madam?' Keshav replied in a polite tone.

She looked out of the window and asked, 'Where are we going?'

'There are a few apartments in Malabar Hill that I am going to show you. All prime properties. You will love them. I am telling you, you'll be confused which one to choose.'

'Don't set such high expectations, Keshav,' She said calmly. She was never used to being calm, and that startled her. Perhaps moving to Mumbai was the right thing to do. She watched more iconic buildings from the old city as the Innova passed by Churchgate station.

'Madam?'

'Yes, Keshav?'

'Would you like some music?'

'No, I am okay. Thanks!'

The driver smiled, hiding his embarrassment. He had hoped that the woman would say yes and break the uncomfortable silence inside the car. As the car moved towards the Netaji Subhash Chandra Bose Road, Anahita saw the end of land approaching.

Marine Drive was one of the most popular spots for both tourists and residents of Mumbai. The cab took another right and entered the long stretch of road known as the Queen's Necklace. It ran for three kilometres and connected Nariman Point with Babulnath.

Anahita could see the sea on her left now, through the car's window. Shallow waves formed and crashed rhythmically in the distance. People of all colours and classes thronged the promenade – some alone and others in groups. Some were selling cotton candy or coffee in little paper cups, while others were cuddling their lovers. A small wave lashed on a rock somewhere and a visual from the past fluttered before her eyes. Two girls were walking down the promenade, one of them startlingly resembling Anahita from nine years ago.

No … no … no. Not those memories, she begged her mind. She closed the window and turned towards the driver. 'Can you please turn on the radio, Keshav?' Anahita's voice quivered as she made the request.

'Yes, of course!' The driver turned on the music system. 'Anything in particular you want, madam?'

'No. Just play whatever you like.'

'Okay,' Keshav said, noting the sudden change in Anahita's behaviour.

'*Beetein Lamhe*' played on the radio. Anahita closed her eyes again. She did not want to think of anything from her past. She had promised her mother that she would never return to Mumbai. That was nine years ago.

---

11 July 2010, Saturday

A rush of warm air from the sea passed placidly and made its way into Anahita's lungs. A subtle view of the calm Arabian Sea soothed her mind. The smell of tobacco fumes and salty water did not hamper the experience. The sun's reflection on the surface of the sea gave it a sparkling silvery appearance.

'You can stop staring at the sea; it will not take you in,' said a voice that sounded like honey melting in a hearth.

'I don't want the sea to gobble me up,' an eighteen-year-old Anahita said with a sly smile on her supple face. 'Mehr, I just wished I could have more control over my life.'

'How is this helping that?' Mehr sipped coffee from a little paper cup. She looked unmoved.

Anahita noticed Mehr's wheatish skin shining under the noon sun. *You look so beautiful, that skin you have; wish I could bury my fingers in it forever.* Anahita's left hand involuntarily moved to touch Mehr's skin, but she pulled herself back. With her eyes fixed on the horizon, Anahita said, 'Staring at the vastness with nothing else to distract helps me calm my thoughts. You know how my thoughts can be all over the place.'

'I know. But you cannot always come here when you feel down or dejected. Especially since you are not going to move to Mumbai. Thanks to your mom – the great Vatsala aunty!'

'It is not that …'

Mehr shook her head. 'I don't know when you and your mom will move on. For God's sake, that thing happened to you because of me!'

'Exactly! And that is why she doesn't like me mingling with you. She felt relieved when you moved to Mumbai after the incident. Besides, I can't turn against my mother. She has gone through a lot because of me.'

'Do you think it was easy for me to move on? You know what I do when the memory of that damned bastard haunts me?' asked Mehr.

'What?'

Mehr's mood immediately changed from frustrated to calm. 'I will tell you. I learnt this from a mindfulness meditation group on Facebook. Try closing your eyes wherever you are. Close it so hard that you devote your brain completely to perform the action, making it unable to generate anymore thoughts until you open your eyes again.'

'I don't think it's going to work.'

'Try it, Anu … Try it!'

Anahita smiled and gave in. She turned and took in a deep breath, and closed her eyes tightly. For a moment, her mind still showed her the sea, then the beautiful face of her friend sitting in the sun, the sound of waves hitting her ear drums. Then it faded to pitch black. The aroma of the coffee wafted into Anahita's nostrils until they reached the alveolar sacs and disappeared as oxygen atoms – that is what she had learnt in Biology class. *Alveolar sacs are cells that exchange oxygen and carbon dioxide in the lungs; the core utility of the breathing process, the process that keeps one alive.* Good air and bad air; that was how her teacher explained oxygen and carbon dioxide before she drew the respiratory cycle on the blackboard. A board that was black (or was it green?). A chalk diagram of alveoli that she had seen in her classroom formed in the blackness of her tightly closed eyes.

No, no. I can't have thoughts.

She tried hard to erase it and go back to the blackness, but the chalk diagram turned into a slimy disintegrating object. Viscous yellow pus started oozing out of it. The pus splattered all over and before she knew it, the yellow turned red – blood red. The red was all over her, and there was a shadow of a large man. Anahita wanted to open her eyes, but she could not. She tried to scream, but her mouth would not even open. *Am I paralyzed?* Anahita pressed her eyelids harder, but it did not help.

Breathe in. Breathe out … Anahita … Breathe!

The visuals faded and blackness took over again. Her eyelids unclenched and she could feel her body relax. With every deep breath, she sensed the *good air* filling up her alveoli and *bad air* pushed out of her system. Peace. Blackness.

Present Day

'Madam?' The driver called from his seat.

When Anahita opened her eyes, she realized she was still in the Innova. The scar above Keshav's eye turned her stomach. For a moment, she thought she was back in that dreaded classroom from August 2005. Keshav had already taken Anahita to see five vacant apartments. She did not like any of them. Some were in noisy areas, some were too big for her. She always fancied living in an ideal high-rise apartment in Mumbai, but none of the houses that she checked satisfied her fancies.

'Would you like to go back to the hotel, madam?'

'Have we been to all the apartments from your list?'

'This is the last one.'

Anahita looked out of the window. The sunlight blinded her momentarily, but she could soon see the towering apartment with grey stone-clad walls. She scanned the building from the top floor to the bottom, where she saw a small board that read Paradise Heights.

Cute name. But why do the buildings look so familiar?

'Many Bollywood movies from the nineties were shot here, Madam,' Keshav said, as if he had read Anahita's thoughts. He exited the car, and walked over to Anahita's door to open it for her.

'Ah, that is probably why I feel like I have seen it before.' Stepping out of the car, she tried to recollect a movie where she might have seen the buildings. 'Maybe in one of those early movies of Rakesh Kapoor. *Sajna ki Doli* … was it?'

'Rakesh Kapoor?' Keshav seemed excited. 'Do you like him?'

'Yes, I am a huge fan.'

A victorious grin blossomed on the driver's face. 'Rakesh dada is a dear friend of Bhau. I think he is going to join Bhau's party this time. He will be the first non-Marathi to contest on an MNP ticket.'

Keshav locked the car and lead Anahita to the elevator. 'Please come, madam.'

On the way, they passed a guard's cabin with a chalky visitor's register, the day's newspaper and an empty chair. There was a monitor on the desk, with live CCTV footage playing. The guard was missing from the scene; perhaps he had gone for a smoke.

The thought that it was an unfamiliar elevator alarmed Anahita. She asked, 'Uh … Can we take the stairs, please?'

Keshav looked surprised. 'It is on the seventh floor.'

'That's okay. I can walk.'

Keshav responded with a smile and strode towards the staircase. He found the woman weird, but parked the thought. He had an apartment to show her.

7

Paradise Heights

Dust covered the maroon living room walls, which gave them a slightly brownish appearance. A teakwood sofa set spread out in an L-shape with a broad table in the centre; a cabinet with lots of space for books and showpieces made up the living room. There were elaborate carvings on the wood that gave the interiors a traditional European look and feel. The smell of ageing wood consumed Anahita's olfactory senses; she did not like it. The ceiling was higher than usual, and that made her feel smaller and trapped. Keshav waited outside as it did not feel right to enter when she was alone inside.

Anahita looked at the maroon curtain that separated the living room from the rest of the apartment. *I should get rid of that ugly thing.* She drew the curtain to one side and felt something sticky clinging to her fingers from the fabric. Once she drew the curtains apart, the living room extended into a larger space that she could use as a dining area. She scanned one corner of the area to the other, traversing from the kitchen door on the left to the three doors that led to different rooms on the right. She heard footsteps in the living room. *Probably Keshav.*

Anahita opened the first door from the right that led to a study room with a large wooden shelf meant for a library or an office room. There were lots of books in the room. The large French windows faced east, and she assumed they gave a magnificent view early in the morning. She pulled the door to shut it and walked to the next one.

The second room looked like a bedroom, but it did not have any furniture like the other ones, just a large window on the Eastern side. The room was a perfect square with the same maroon painted walls.

Who would paint their walls maroon? Anahita wondered as she closed the door and looked at the ceiling, walking over to the third door. She turned the knob, but it was jammed. She jiggled it, but the knob wouldn't budge.

Maybe it needs more strength or a key?

'Keshav?'

After a few minutes of radio silence, Anahita turned around and was about to walk out of the place when she heard a small clatter behind her. Instinctively, she turned back towards the door. It was now ajar. A putrid odour wafted out through the gap. Absent-mindedly, Anahita nudged the door open and entered the large rectangular bedroom. There was a vintage writing desk on the left, while a beautiful cot dominated the room. Unlike the other rooms, this one was purple and there were patches of paint peeling off the wall. She felt at ease at once, as if an invisible force was putting her to sleep; a warm touch that promised to show beautiful dreams if she closed her eyes. The feeling that one would get moments before an afternoon siesta. She liked the room. There was a bedside table. She had already decided that she would keep her favourite photo-collage on that table. No, it was as if the photo always belonged there. Anahita reeled with a sense of déjà vu.

I must have been here before. Did I come here for an ad shoot? Was it that short film where I played a part? Did I come here with Mehr on one of those parties and got so drunk that I woke up in my hotel room or her bedroom? How can I forget something that happened only as recently as nine years ago? Has my anxiety disorder eaten so deeply into my cognitive abilities that I can't recollect from memory?

Her left eye welled up, the right one almost on the brink. *Just breathe.*

Anahita wiped the tear and glanced at the dark-coloured curtain on the eastern side. She pulled it to reveal a glass door that opened to the balcony. It was then that she realized it had become very cloudy outside. It could rain any moment. The glass door had an old-style latch.

Behind her, she felt someone move. Warm breath fell on her bare skin, just below her neck. *Who … ?*

'You must leave,' a male voice echoed in the empty room.

Anahita turned. It was Keshav. He was standing with a phone in his hand. 'Your husband just called, madam. We must go back and pick him from the office. Are you done here?'

'Yes. Yes, in fact I was about to come out,' Anahita told the driver. 'Let us go.'

Anahita Anand and Keshav exited the room. The door closed behind them and, unbeknownst to them, so did the curtain on the glass door.

8

⁓

Bhau's Study

EVERY NIGHT, BHAU SPENT THIRTY MINUTES ALONE IN his study, contemplating the events of the day and the years that had gone by, with nothing but the music of Bhupendra Singh playing in his old tape recorder and a glass of whiskey in his hand. While Singh's voice hauntingly chanted '*Dil Dhoondta Hain*' from the stereo speakers of the Panasonic RQ-2755 tape recorder, Bhau closed his eyes and pictured visuals from the talkie of a bygone era. Thunder raged outside in the night sky. The ice cubes in the whiskey jazzed rhythmically as his hand moved with the song's tune.

At the end of the song, the cassette player stopped with a thud – a side had ended. So had his thirty minutes of contemplation. Someone knocked on the door. He rose from the sofa with the glass in his hand. 'Come in.' Bhau stopped at the bar to pour himself another drink.

Keshav opened the door and entered. He looked tired from the day's trips. He greeted his master, his role model.

'What happened, Keshav? Why do you look so worried?' Bhau spoke in Marathi that had a deep Varhadi accent.

Keshav replied in the local version of their mother tongue, 'I took the woman to see the houses.'

'Good. Did she like any?'

'Well …' Keshav hesitated.

'Tell me, Keshav. What is it?'

'She liked 7E, the apartment in Paradise Heights.'

'What?' Bhau appeared thunderstruck. 'Why did you show her that house? You know that nobody would want to live in a house with such a dark past.'

'Bhau, I … I did not think that she would like it. I just showed it as it was on the way.' Keshav's eyes were full of guilt and fear. 'I am really sorry. I will tell her tomorrow that the house is not available.'

Bhau took a moment to come to terms with the driver's revelation. Finally, he said, 'It is okay. I think it is time we let go of the past. The house has been locked for almost twenty-one years now. Whatever ghost of the past it contained must have died away. A new tenant will help everyone forget about it.' Bhau looked at his loyal driver and handy-man and said, 'Clean the house and ask our guests to make themselves comfortable, as long as they have to live in Mumbai. Understand?'

'Yes, Bhau.' Keshav nodded with the obedience of a child.

'Goodnight, Keshav.'

As Keshav exited the room, Bhau changed the side of the cassette and pressed *play*. Another classic started. He lifted the glass of whisky and gulped it. He needed an extra thirty minutes to contemplate that night.

'Naam Gum Jaayega … Chehra Yeh Badal Jaayega …'

9

7 August 2019, Wednesday
The Indie, Versova

EVERY EMPLOYEE IN THAT SMALL SQUARE-SHAPED OFFICE in the peripheries of Mumbai feared the wrath of their editor, Mehrab Hussain. With most offices in the area being casting agencies and studios, *The Indie* was an odd one out. It was an independent online news portal. With the emergence of the world wide web and social media, online news portals started mushrooming all over the world; a few of them were funded by conventional news agencies, while the big brands bought others to use them as mouthpieces. Mehrab started *The Indie* with high hopes. It had the distinction of having only female staff members; she was very particular about that. She also swore not to depend on advertisers for an income. However, she went nearly bankrupt paying her employees, until one of MNP's loyalists decided to fund the publication.

Every day thousands of aspiring actors arrived in Mumbai, ending up at casting agencies for auditions. A select few got their breaks, some survived by doing odd jobs, but a major chunk of the crowd simply ended up with heartbreaks – or worse. Girls were even more vulnerable. When she was only fifteen, Mehrab came to Mumbai with her parents to continue her education after a disastrous incident at her previous school in Gurugram. In Mumbai, she wanted to start over. In junior college, she started modelling and her dream grew into ambitions. But the dream also brought her face to face with some of the most notorious sexual predators in the industry. After a series of adversities, Mehrab decided to unmask the rampant exploitation under all the glitz. She did a few sting operations that exposed a few big television stars in 2013. Eventually, she realized her actual passion and became an investigative journalist. After working with some known news channels, she broke off and started her independent news portal – The Indie. She worked from the studio building where she had done her first sting operation.

When Mehrab Hussain's Corolla pulled over in front of the office, every person who was on a break rushed inside. They sat in front of their computers, staring at the screens. Hussain strode into the office and into her cabin. *Relief for the staff.* Sahil Sheikh, a popular filmmaker from Patna, had been waiting for the boss.

'Hi, Mr Sheikh! Sorry to keep you waiting for so long. Do you want me to get you another coffee?' Mehrab offered, glancing at the empty mug on the table in front of her guest.

Sahil Sheikh's eyes stayed on the editor as she walked towards her cushiony executive chair. 'That is okay, Ms Hussain. I just thought I will meet you before I leave for London. My flight is in two hours.'

'Oh, a cab will get you there in thirty minutes. Tell me, how can I help you?'

'You see, I follow your newsbreaks on the internet. I even follow you on Twitter.'

'That is very supportive of you. We try to report independent news. Did you come here to tell me this, Mr Sahil Sheikh?' She stared at the man, and he understood that she wanted him to come to the point.

'Recently, your website had done some reports linking superstar Binay with the Me Too campaign based on some third-class model's rants. Binay is the biggest superstar in our industry and my movie with him releases in a couple of weeks. Your campaign is hurting my movie's prospects.'

'What?'

'I have pumped a lot of money into this movie. Fans love Binay and they will make it a success for sure, but all this controversy is making him less popular among girls. You understand? I will lose money. You can do all this after three or for months, you know.'

'Your *hero* talks of woman empowerment on screen, and off screen he is just another piece of misogynistic crap. There is no way in hell I will stop this campaign.' Mehrab pulled out her mobile phone, opened Twitter and started typing. 'What is your Twitter handle? No need, you are famous enough; I can search.' As she typed, Mehrab's fingers trembled with an unsettling rage, but the man in the room did not seem to notice it. An uncomfortable silence in the room preceded the sound of a notification on Sahil's mobile phone. He unlocked the screen and saw the tweet from @TheIndieOfficial.

'Can't compromise the #Metoo for MCP scavengers like you @sahilfilmmaker81. U r not welcome in my office. U & ur superstar are going down. FO!'

The filmmaker could not figure out what MCP and FO meant, but he gathered the gist of the tweet. Before he could react, Mehrab spoke, 'I believe you did not do your homework before making an appointment with me. Now, get out of here before my head explodes.'

'You shameless woman, people talk to me with respect. I have made ten blockbusters in my career.' Sahil got up in rage. He leaned across the table threateningly.

Mehrab seemed unaffected. 'Don't you understand what FO means?' She motioned towards the door and then flipped her middle finger at him. 'Fuck off!'

Sheikh's eyes turned red as he put all his effort into controlling himself. He clenched his fist and stormed out of the room, carrying his bruised ego with him.

Such episodes were not new to the editor and her staff. Hussain had a clear-cut policy for her campaign exposé: once she had a grip on a predator, she would not let go until she had strangled him. Like the vulture that cleans up rotting corpses, Mehrab felt it was her duty to wipe off the corrupt ones in power.

Back in her cabin, Mehrab shook her head vigorously and then did something with her hand that looked like herding out negative energy invisible to the eye. A couple of timid knocks on the door brought her back to reality. 'Come in.' An aged man wearing a khadi kurta and white pyjamas entered with his signature *jhola*. As soon as Ms Hussain saw his withered face, she felt sorry for the ancient journalist who had not kept up with the times.

'Amol ji. What a surprise!' Mehrab could not believe that an old-school journalist like Amol Abhyankar would ever step inside a modern web-based news portal's office. For a long time, he refused to accept that journalism had moved on to the internet and social media.

'Mehrab beta, I know you would have never expected me in your office, but I am here because nobody else would let me in,' he said. His frail voice betrayed his regret and grief.

He was one of the best investigative reporters of his time, back in the early nineties when even cable television was not common in India, forget about social media. In the process, he upset some powerful men and a fake corruption case tainted his pristine career and eventually ended up with him serving jail time. By the time he was released, the world had moved on to satellite and digital news, and Amol's form of journalism existed only in digitized archives of public libraries. Aware of how much weight he would have carried twenty years back, Mehrab Hussain humbly welcomed him. 'Tell me. How can I help you?'

The aged journalist sighed. 'Nobody likes the good old unbiased story anymore. Everyone is working for one big guy or the other. I just had some stories, I thought, you know … maybe you guys would be interested.'

Mehrab had expected something like this. Abhyankar had been trying to dispose of his old investigation stories and reports to digital news websites, since the bigger media houses firmly refused to take them. His stories were all dated.

'Is there anything recent among them?' Hussain asked, already starting to regret letting the old man inside.

'Not really. But all the stories I have are sensational – *conspiracies!*'

'*Were* sensational. If you have anything recent, then I promise you I will publish them. But if they are stuff from the nineties, then I can't.' Mehrab Hussain threw her hands in the air. 'My readers are mostly young adults who were not even born at the time of your reports. I hope you understand.'

'I understand.' Abhyankar rose from the chair. 'I will not waste any more of your precious time.'

Mehrab felt a jab of guilt. Abhyankar smiled to put her at ease. 'I appreciate whatever you have been doing here, Mehr beta. You are a fearless journalist who isn't afraid to question those in power. Remember, someday, you will also be tested. And when that time comes, you must choose the right side.'

10

7 August 2019, Wednesday
7E, Paradise Heights

THE LARGE CURTAIN IN THE LIVING ROOM CAME fluttering to the floor. Varun tried to roll the fabric into a lump, but when it did not cooperate, he folded it and handed it to Anahita.

'I did not like this colour at all, thanks for taking it down.' Anahita dumped the curtain into a large cardboard carton with other things discarded from the old décor, things the new occupants did not care for.

'We don't have to keep these. In fact, we can get rid of everything,' Varun said. He dragged a chair over, and standing on it, he stretched and reached out to take down the curtain rod.

'Well, I like the couch and that bookshelf in the library. The furniture just needs dusting, and they will be good as new. I think those might be vintage items.'

'It belonged to the previous tenant. I am just assuming.'

'Was it your client? What did Keshav call him? Bhau?'

'Yes, Bhau. I do not know if he lived here or not, because he owns over a dozen properties in this area. He uses some of his properties as accommodation for his guests, like us. Others he rents to VIPs. Keshav told me that the rent from such places supports Bhau's orphanage.'

'Oh! That is so kind of him.'

'Well, he is super rich and powerful,' Varun said, thinking back to the tumbler of tea in his office. 'They've got to maintain that image. Besides, the boys from the orphanage grow to become his loyal lackeys.'

'Like Keshav?'

Varun nodded, getting down from the chair and putting it back in place. 'All I know is that he will make me richer by a few crores by the end of 2020, and next year we will be holidaying in Switzerland.' Without the curtain, the living room looked bland but bright. Varun turned to his wife. 'This room looks done. Shall we go to the kitchen and unpack other items?'

The two made their way to the kitchen. Items wrapped in packing material littered the otherwise empty space. Anahita glanced at the unpacked OTG box, her fingers itching with excitement at the thought of baking. Varun had wanted to get their old microwave from Delhi, but Anahita insisted on buying a new OTG instead. She did not get her cakes right with microwaves.

In one of the cartons, Varun found Anahita's photo-collage, filled with pictures from different stages of her life — from the time she stood first in the second grade to the day she married Varun. She always kept the collage next to her bed in the old house in Gurugram. Varun handed it to Anahita. She went to the bedroom and placed it on the bedside table. On her way back to the living room, Anahita's eyes scanned the ceiling. There was seepage; tiny bits of limestone scrapes from the ceiling fell off like snow, remained suspended in the air for a while, and then mixed with the air that Anahita was breathing in … setting inside the alveolar sac. *Alveolar sac. Alveolar sacs are cells that exchange oxygen and carbon dioxide in the lungs; the core utility of the breathing process, the process that keeps one alive. Good air and bad air.* She saw the seepage pattern rearrange itself into the diagram of alveolar sac.

'There! Everything is ready. The kitchen is all yours!' Varun called out as he looked at his reflection on the polished black surface of the stove. He noticed his wife staring blankly at the seepage on the ceiling. 'Anu?'

'Haan?'

Anahita snapped out of the reverie; the seepage looked abstract once again. She noticed that her husband had unpacked everything in the kitchen: the stove, OTG, the pans, and utensils … everything was already in the cabinet. 'When did you do all this?'

'Mm. In the last ten minutes while you were staring at the ceiling.'

Ten minutes? Was I staring at that thing for ten minutes? I really need to get some rest now. Anahita rubbed her fingers against each other, slowly.

'Are you all right, dear?'

'Yes.' She felt an inexplicable unease.

'Do you want me to book a Skype appointment with Dr Malhotra?'

'No, that won't be necessary.' Anahita's fingers fidgeted behind her back. Varun grabbed her right hand to ease the anxiety. 'I will take a nap,' she said.

'All right.'

As she walked out of the kitchen, Varun said, 'I will call you at four. We have to leave for a party at six.'

'Party?'

'Yeah. Bhau has invited us over for his mother's birthday party.'

'Why didn't you tell me before?' Anahita stared at her husband accusingly.

'I must have forgotten. I am sorry, but we *have* to go. Can't disappoint the new client.'

'Well, then *you have to* go to the party. I will stay home.'

'Actually, Bhau has specially asked me to bring you along. I could not say no.'

'You can tell him I am on my periods. I am sure that he would not want a menstruating woman around him; at least that is what I heard his party stood for.'

'Come on, darling! It is not a religious ritual. He specifically mentioned that it was a party. Can't you do this for me, just once? How long has it been since we went out together? I won't drag you to any other parties after this. Besides, you will also get to meet new people there – Bollywood actors, politicians from his party, cricketers, socialites. You might not want to miss this opportunity.'

Anahita saw a glint in his eye and wondered if that was the right time to bargain. What if she told him she was pregnant with his child? Will her going to that party make the news easier? Probably not, but she decided to at least lay the groundwork for breaking the news.

'I will come to your party, but you owe me a favour. You won't say no to it, no matter what I ask of you.'

'I give you my word.'

Well, that was easy. I hope the day of revelation goes just as smoothly.

11

❧

Later that evening

THERE WERE ABOUT A HUNDRED VERY IMPORTANT people attending Renuka Deshmukh's eightieth birthday celebration at Bhau's farmhouse. The guests had drinks in their hands, mingled with one another, exchanged pleasantries. One could not tell by looking at them if the people were glad to see each other, but that is what they would say, with a smile plastered on their faces.

Anahita and Varun arrived at quarter to eight in Keshav's Innova. While parking, Keshav informed them that the BMW in front of them belonged to Bollywood superstar Rakesh Kapoor. Anahita, who had little reason to be at the party except for a bargain, felt excited when she finally saw her favourite actor coming out of the car. She wanted to shake his hand, get an autograph or a selfie, but hesitated to approach. The actor and his wife walked by them, paying no attention to Anahita, the *fan*.

Maybe I should have stayed in Mumbai. I might have been an actress. Maybe he would have noticed me, talked to me.

Keshav opened the door for her. She looked splendid in her white evening gown, and the pearl necklace adorning her slender neck made her look like a Disney princess – beautiful but meek, pretty but frail. Varun looked dashing in his white tuxedo and trousers. When Varun escorted Anahita inside, the couple grabbed quite a few eyeballs. Some guests wanted to know who the young unseen faces were. On the outside, they looked like a dream couple. But Anahita knew Varun wasn't as enthusiastic as he had been four years ago, when he had proposed to her. She still remembered that afternoon of 14 March: Varun deliberately chose not to wish Anahita on her birthday and, worse, cancelled their date citing an urgent official duty. He told her he would be flying off to Bangalore to meet a prospective client and would not be back until a month later. Anahita wanted to meet him before he left, but he refused. And then suddenly, even as she was fuming with rage, Anahita received a call from Varun at exactly twelve in the night. At first, she did not answer. But the phone rang relentlessly. When she picked up, hoping to hear Varun's voice, a woman spoke instead, claiming to be a police officer. The previous call made from Varun's phone number was to Anahita, and therefore, the officer had called to inquire if she could identify the *body*. Anahita froze. There had been an accident near Mahipalpur, and they found the phone in the victim's pocket. Anahita's eyes filled to the brim, and she wrapped a shawl around her, picked up the scooty's key and sprinted to the door. When she opened it, there he stood, towering in front of her in that very white tuxedo and a silky black shirt and trousers. Varun Anand in flesh and blood.

Anahita went through emotions at the speed of light – shock, at seeing a supposedly dead man at her door; confusion, as her mind started wavering and she doubted her sanity – *am I seeing things again*; and then overwhelmed tears. But before she could break down completely, Varun held her tightly in his arms and informed her he was okay, that he just wanted to surprise her. He slid something over the ring finger of her left hand. A diamond ring! And then he revealed his actual intentions. Anahita hugged him tightly, all other feelings but absolute joy fading into the background. Anahita realized one thing that night – she cared dearly for Varun. She always thought she was incapable of loving a man, but Varun had changed her mind and heart. Varun, who had a crush on Anahita for many months, got a 'yes' in reply on her birthday.

Four years had passed since then, and now she was staring at the diamond ring; it had not worn off, unlike their marriage. She was now just a wife to a man whose life revolved around an ambitious career. She blamed her genophobia for most of the problems. *Don't let these people see your troubles. Smile!*

At a distance, Bhau was chatting with a friend when he noticed Varun and the beautiful woman with him. 'Welcome, welcome Varun, to my humble abode,' he said.

As Varun walked up to him, Bhau introduced him to another man, 'Godbole, this is Varun Anand. He is a master planner of election campaigns. He is the reason Ravinder Aggarwal is Delhi's chief minister. Varun is a Raavan!'

'Hello, Mr Deshmukh, Mr Godbole.'

'Everyone calls me Bhau.' Bhau smiled and introduced his colleague. 'Godbole is the Commissioner of Police. If you get into trouble with anything in my city, he is your go-to guy.'

Varun smiled and shook hands with the commissioner. 'Pleased to meet you, sir.'

Bhau turned to the young and beautiful Anahita. 'This must be your lovely wife.'

'Hello sir!' Anahita greeted him in a timid voice. Her hands trembled a little as she folded them into a 'namaste'.

The politician patted Anahita's head, like a father blessing his daughter. 'I am so glad that you came.' He looked at the young woman. She appeared unnerved and the smile on her face didn't do much to hide it. 'We have arranged a fine performance from superstar Rakesh Kapoor for the ladies tonight,' He pointed at the patio where many women were sitting, waiting eagerly for the country's favourite superstar. 'Why don't you join them while I borrow your husband?'

'Of course.'

Bhau gestured for a server to escort Anahita to the patio. Anahita accepted the service and proceeded.

'So, are you ready to meet my nephew?' asked Bhau, his right arm now around Varun's shoulder.

'Yes!' Varun hid his discomfort at Bhau's informal behaviour.

Godbole took his leave and joined another friend. That left Varun and Bhau with each other. Varun had pictured Bhau as the stringent and fanatic leader who lacked compassion and only meant business, and he confirmed that impression after his meeting with the senior leader earlier at the office. But now, he wondered if anything was really how it seemed from the outside. It made him think of his marriage. *No, things are never how they look on the outside.*

12

Varun had imagined Abhinav Deshmukh as a promising personality – smart, knowledgeable, quiet, eloquent. When Varun met him, however, he realized that the heir to the throne wasn't anything like it. Unlike his paternal uncle, Abhinav was short, fairer in complexion, with spiked hair and round eyes on his oval-shaped face. The stubble did not give him the manly appearance expected of a powerful man's only nephew. In fact, he looked like a baby, and babies were not to be taken seriously in politics. Varun had deciphered all this in the first minute of meeting him, when Bhau introduced them to each other. The body language was not correct. He slouched on his cushioned seat with a stooped back, unlike his uncle, who always sat erect with his ankle resting on his knee. Abhinav had too casual a voice for a man of twenty-eight. The Constitution allows an Indian citizen above twenty-five years of age to become the chief minister of any state if he or she is a member of the state legislature or can *buy* permission from the governor. So, yes, Abhinav was *eligible*, but the question was whether the brat was *suitable*. Varun realized how difficult the job at hand would be. *This baby-face is not 'chief minister' material*, Varun thought, as he listened to his client in the room adorned with modern art. The walls did not allow the noise from outside to percolate inside the room.

'I will do whatever you ask me to do. Okay, dada? But you must do a great social media campaign for me. I think that is where we will get the pulse of the youth.' The baby-face spoke with feigned confidence that was betrayed by nervousness with which he shifted in his seat.

'Of course. In fact, I channelled 30 per cent of the total money into social media. Twitter, especially, is a medium where we can set trolls on a roll.' In his mind, Varun kept wondering how long it would take for the opposition to set their trolls firing on Abhinav's words of wisdom. What Varun really wanted to ask was, *Do you even want to be the next CM of Maharashtra or is your uncle pushing you into the abyss to keep the dynasty from collapsing?*

'I am sure that the people will shower me with the same affection that my uncle has received in all these years,' Abhinav said.

Varun smiled with a hint of reluctance. A few months ago, when Varun had started his ambitious pursuit, his ex-employer had told him about the Dunning-Kruger effect. He called Varun an overconfident youngster for giving up a well-paid job in an MNC. In essence, what happens when people believe they are smarter than they really are, a cognitive bias in people with low abilities. Such people do not realize their own incompetence. His boss's prophecy was eventually proven wrong and fortune favoured Varun in the end. But Varun wondered what his ex-boss would say today about him meeting with Maharashtra's most powerful man and his over-confident nephew.

To Abhinav, Varun said, 'My social media team is already working on a strategy for you.' He flicked open a report on his phone and showed it to Bhau and Abhinav. As Abhinav went through the report, Varun said, 'What we noticed is that your followers on Instagram are mostly females in the age group of thirteen to seventeen. Now that might be a glorious thing to boast about, but they will not vote for you in this election – they can't. They will be a good bet for the elections in 2024; for now, they may influence their parents or elders. We need to focus on the age groups eighteen to twenty-four and twenty-five to thirty-one mainly. It is very easy to influence the former category, because they are politically less aware than those above thirty.'

'Is it? But youngsters are pretty woke these days. They know their shit,' Abhinav said, returning the phone to Varun. His carefree tone revealed his own lack of awareness.

'Varun is correct, Abhinav,' the minister intervened. 'Youngsters think they know a lot about politics, but they are vulnerable to manipulation.'

'We call it Dunning-Kruger effect,' Varun said.

Abhinav quickly Googled the term on his phone. 'Oh yeah. Bang on!' He looked at his uncle with an approving smile. 'Chachu, I think we have got the best man to look after my campaign.' He turned to Varun. 'I am all yours, bro!'

'I am glad that you find me capable.'

Varun's calm and positive attitude impressed Bhau. The elder politician knew his nephew would not be easy to mould into a politician, but he had confidence in Varun's abilities.

'From this moment onwards,' continued Varun, 'I will monitor your activities, personally. No press interactions. You must post nothing on social media without getting my approval. We are going to capitalize on the patriotic flavour of the season and launch your campaign on fifteenth of August. In fact, my team will share a strategy document with you soon. A detailed list of content that we will post on your social media handles. Other than that, you will not express your opinions at any public event. You will only say what we tell you to. You will confine your private life to the walls of your bedroom. I hope you are with me,' Varun spoke with authority.

Abhinav switched glances between his uncle and Varun. Bhau nodded in an assuring manner, which convinced Abhinav.

'Yeah, I am with you, bro,' said Abhinav.

Varun grinned. 'Well, we will rock this election. Break a leg or two, or maybe an entire coalition.'

'Oh, damn that cursed coalition! We need to win on our own and we need a solid *mudda*. Our motive. What is it going to be, Varun? Corruption? Electricity? Fuel price? Inflation?'

A moment of silence followed as Varun allowed the anticipation to build. Varun got up from his seat and walked up to the wall where a painting was on display. Bhau waited keenly for the master strategist's answer. The picture of a globe with knives plunged into it – a statement on the ecological destruction of the earth – made for an impactful backdrop behind Varun as he turned and looked over his shoulder, eyed the painting, and then looking back at the ex-chief minister, declared, 'Environment!'

13

Rakesh Kapoor did his regular dance moves for the audience that largely comprised of middle-aged women. Renuka Deshmukh, Bhau's octogenarian mother, was a huge admirer of the Bollywood superstar. She strongly believed that Rakesh was the most charming actor in the Hindi film industry after Dilip Kumar and Dharmendra. The actor invited the birthday *girl* on stage. She danced to one of his latest hits. Anahita sat somewhere in the back without company. She recognized a few faces; faces that appeared in women's magazines and television debates. There was that lady who had jumped her political party and joined Bhau's *dal* because of rampant sexism in the former. *What was her name? Oh, yeah! Mansi Chakravarthy.* Mansi was a spokesperson for the Maharashtra Nationalist Party now and appeared on prime-time debates supporting ultra-nationalist views, which were not hers. Rakesh had been campaigning for Bhau for quite some time and was getting a ticket in the upcoming elections. With him on the party's side, all the women between thirty and fifty would vote for MNP. *Varun will rely on this*, Anahita thought. As another song started playing, she looked for some companionship, a friendly face. There was none.

Isolation crept into her mind. She wondered how long Varun would take as she started getting the urge to go home. It was a strange new place, and she feared it would trigger an anxiety attack any moment. Her head ached, as did her back. It felt as if bubbles of acid were exploding inside her stomach, hurting the soft lining of the intestines. The muscles expanded and contracted; her heart pounded so loudly that she could not hear the song's beats anymore. A sudden realization hit her. *No! No! No! I can't get periods. I am pregnant.*

Anahita excused herself from the crowd. She found the women's restroom in the corner. A well-lit and neatly maintained western setup, mostly white, like the party office. Anahita was on a diet suggested by her Ayurvedic nutritionist; she ingested nothing with excess *pitha*. She was not even drinking cold water because that could heat the body. What had gone wrong? Was it the flight she took from Delhi or the flight of stairs that she had been going up and down at her new apartment? She prayed as she pulled down her underwear and checked for spotting. Nothing! She sighed. Silence.

Then a drop of thick brown blood dropped on the white tiled floor. And then another one and another. She gasped for breath, her heart skipping several beats. Before she knew it, the entire floor had turned brownish red. A weird smell enveloped her; she felt it *hitting the alveoli*. A diagram of the cellular sac started appearing on the blood, but in a darker shade.

Try closing your eyes wherever you are. Close it so hard that you devote your brain completely to perform the action, making it unable to generate any thoughts until you open your eyes again.

Anahita closed her eyes, took deep breaths until she could feel the darkness cocoon her. The pain in her tummy reduced as she put more pressure on her eyelids. The heart relaxed. With slow trembling breath, she opened her eyes. There was no blood on the floor, not even a spot. She had imagined it. A sigh of relief!

When Anahita emerged from the restroom, her clothes were sweaty, but she had combed her hair back to how they were when she arrived at the party.

Just keep calm. You are fine. Just remember what Dr Malhotra had advised. Just remember what Mehr had said.

Someone called out her name from behind, 'Anu?' Anahita recognized that voice. She had last heard it years ago, yet it haunted her every night in the deepest of dreams. Anahita turned and stood in shock, for she was seeing this person after nine years … 'Mehr!' *Am I imagining her too, or is she here for real?* Anahita would have even pinched herself to check if Mehr had not come forward and clutched her palms.

'Wow … You are here!' Mehr said, hugging Anahita. Her voice had not changed. It had that honey-like viscous texture even now, just a lot firmer.

'Yes. I … I also did not expect to see you here, tonight. I mean … Obviously! I knew you would be in Mumbai. But here? This is a surprise.' Anahita smiled, a little embarrassed, especially since she did not want to reveal what she had gone through moments ago.

'You look tired. Is everything okay?' Mehr inquired.

'Just not having a splendid night. All these unfamiliar faces.'

'Of course, I can understand. Even I'm here under a sort of obligation.'

'What kind of obligation?'

'Well, Bhau's friend started funding my company when it went bankrupt. So, I had to come since he invited. What about you? How did you end up at this boring party?'

'Mr Deshmukh is my husband's client.'

'Husband? Oh, when did that happen?'

'Four years ago.'

Mehr allowed the news to sink in, and then came closer to her friend and examined the glow on her face. 'That is a pleasant scent you are wearing.'

Before Anahita could respond, she saw Varun approaching them. She nodded at Mehr and placed a finger on the lips. Mehr turned and noticed the suited man; instinctively, she knew this was the husband.

'There you are. I was looking for you at the patio,' Varun said, smiling at his wife.

'Oh, I just came to use the restroom,' Anahita replied.

When Varun glanced at Mehr, a total stranger for him, Anahita introduced her friend to her husband. 'This is Mehr, my … *friend*.' A tinge of sorrow echoed in the words. 'And Mehr, this is my husband, Varun.'

Varun and Mehr shook hands. *Quite a powerful grip for a woman*, Varun thought. 'I am glad that you found an old friend, darling. Mehr, you should come over to our place. We are living in Malabar Hill.'

'Oh? Me too. Where in Malabar Hill?'

'Paradise Heights, 7E,' Varun told her. Behind him, Anahita stayed silent, her fingers fidgeting.

'Ah! That one, eh? Beautiful view.'

'Are you done for the night, Varun?' Anahita asked, suddenly ignoring Mehr's presence.

'Yes.'

'Can we go home? I am not feeling well.'

'Sure, let us go.' He turned to Mehr. 'It was nice meeting you.'

'Likewise.' Mehr smiled formally. 'Take care, Anu … *Anahita*.'

'You too. Goodbye!'

Mehr watched the two disappear into the night, just like it had happened nine years ago. Only then, it had happened at Marine drive. A much younger Anahita had walked out of Mehr's life because she did not have the guts to stand up for herself. Back then, it was her mother and now it was a husband. Mehr felt sorry for Anahita.

14

Midnight, Paradise Heights

The twenty-storey apartment building stood under the swivelling blankets of dark grey clouds. Bursts of lightning exploded occasionally somewhere far away, but the sound mildly diffused into the walls of the bedroom. The weather was exactly the kind horror writers have overused in literature and cinema, but it still managed to spook people out, probably because of something deeply embedded in human genes. When humans were still hunters and gatherers, growling and gnarling to communicate, they feared the dark and rain got them soggy and sick to the core. There were no antibiotics back then. So, early humans watched their weaker companions cough to death; they saw merciless bolts of lightning from above roast branches of trees. They realized that the rain was not a friend and hid inside caves and under rocks. This fear of the dark and of thunder and lightning has stayed with humans till date – like a phobia. Anahita had a phobia of almost everything: enclosed spaces, crowded places, heights, darkness, spiders, speaking to strangers, germs, sexual intercourse. But she was a sucker for rainy nights – *pluviophilia*, it was called. The rain kept her company in solitude.

Usually, she would find it difficult to fall asleep in unfamiliar places, but that night she felt tired. Maybe it was hormonal. She slept beside her husband, her right arm wrapped over his bare chest. Her eyes twitched. She turned in her sleep, lifting her arm from her husband's body, and placing it under her cheek. Anahita murmured; she was dreaming of the past.

13 August 2005, Saturday
Good Shepherd Convent, Gurugram

The people of Gurugram were witnessing one of the wettest Augusts in years. Schools shut down for a week because of the endless rain. The grand construction sites on Mehrauli-Gurgaon road took a hit. The city's infrastructure came tumbling down. When schools re-opened in the second week of August, not everyone made it for the first few days as most of the faculty and students were down with a viral fever.

In the ninth grade, only twelve out of thirty-six students attended. Fourteen-year-old Anahita and her best friend, Mehr, sat on the first bench. Mehr did not want to sit there, but the teacher shifted them to the front because the class was nearly empty.

'Why don't you all come closer and occupy the first two rows,' Mrs Shelly, the sixty-something biology teacher, instructed in a thick accent that immediately gave away the influence of the musical Malayalam spoken in Kerala's Thrissur district. Mrs Shelly touched the ruler kept on the lecturer's table behind her. The students, seven boys and five girls, did not waste any time in obeying her command. Even though two-thirds of the class was absent, the teacher went ahead with the curriculum. She wrote on the board: *Respiratory System* and started drawing a figure with a piece of chalk. With little enthusiasm, the children silently began to copy the diagram onto their notebooks. One boy whispered something to the boy sitting next to him, and they started giggling.

'Christopher?' Mrs Shelly stopped, chalk still touching the blackboard, and turned around. Her brows were furrowed, half-hidden by the frames of her spectacles; she knew that the boy had made fun of her accent. 'What's so funny? Share it with the class, come on.'

The boy made a puckered face. 'Ma'am, we wanted to know … ' He looked at his friends and then finished with a mischievous wink ' … When will you give us a lecture on the human reproductive system?' The class broke into laughter; a couple of girls blushed.

The biology teacher threw the chalk at the boy. 'In class tenth. That is, if you can make it to the next grade. Now get out of my class.'

The chalk had hit Christopher's forehead and left an angry mark right next to the evil-looking scar above his left eye. He giggled again and departed victoriously. Mrs Shelly knew that the punishment would not affect his morale; as long as he had girls giggling at his comments, he would be encouraged to continue. The teacher picked up a new piece of chalk and returned the blackboard.

Mehr twirled her braided hair and looked questioningly at her best friend. 'Seriously yaar, can't Shelly aunty give us a free period today!'

Anahita did not respond; she was focused on the lecture.

'Anahita. Can't you cram it from the textbook? You don't have to be such a teacher's pet!'

Anahita sighed. 'What do you want?'

A sly smile came over Mehr's face. Anahita recognized it very well, and she did not like it.

'Today, if my mom calls you, please tell her I am staying with you. Tell her we are doing group study for the half-yearly exams.' Mehr's request had a commanding tone.

'Are you coming to my place after school? Why didn't you tell me before?'

'No, dumbo! I won't be coming to your place. I have plans. I need an alibi, that's all.'

'No, Mehr. I am not doing this for you.'

'Oh, come on! I am going out with Chris.' Mehr glanced at the boy outside the classroom, who returned her gaze with a wink.

'Bully Christopher?' Anahita said, her face contorted in disgust.

'Please yaar, do this for me. This is the last time, please.' Mehr pinched Anahita's cheek. 'You can't say no to me, yaar.'

'I am telling you this boy is going to get you in trouble. Don't you get bad vibes just looking at that scar? Besides, I hate covering for you all the time.'

'Done! This is the last time.'

Anahita grunted disapprovingly. 'Will you please let me listen to the lecture now?'

'Sure!'

Mehr sat back on the bench, relaxed. Anahita turned her attention back to the teacher.

'Alveolar sacs are cells that exchange oxygen and carbon dioxide in the lungs … ' the teacher drew bubble-shaped objects on the board. 'The core utility of the breathing process, which keeps one alive. Would someone like to complete this diagram for me?' She turned towards the students.

The students tried to dodge the bullet by looking here and there or at their respective desks. No hands except for Anahita's. Mrs Shelly beckoned her and handed her the chalk. At the blackboard, Anahita studied the diagram. Then she chose a vacant area on the board and started drawing – one large circle on the left and a symmetric one right next to it, and more. Before she could finish the drawing, a bell rang, and the teenagers jumped from the seats with joy and relief. It irritated the teacher. She turned to the class, picking up her register and textbook from the table, and announced, 'I know you sleepyheads were looking forward to the zero period but when you come tomorrow, make sure you have revised this diagram of alveolar sacs, and how they help good air reach our lungs. All right?'

'Yes, ma'am!' the students replied in a melancholic chorus.

Mrs Shelly exited the room, looking distastefully at Christopher, who was still standing outside. The moment she left, he dashed in. The students were already packing and leaving for their zero period, which was meant for extra-curricular activities in the ground and basement areas of the school. Since Anahita was not really into any extra-curricular activity, she stayed back in the vacant classroom to do her assignment.

Anahita liked solitude. Since the classroom was on the top floor, the terrace was right above the class's ceiling. The sound of raindrops falling on the terrace echoed inside the empty classroom. She looked out through the paned glass window. Not much was visible because water trickled over the surface. It made everything beyond look blurry. It was perfect. Some figure with a black umbrella was moving on the school ground. *Must be the peon or the gatekeeper.* She came back to her desk, picked up her biology textbook and walked towards the board. She compared the diagram on the board with the figure in the book. Only minor differences. She picked up a duster to wipe the mistakes and began the correction with a piece of chalk. Anahita dreamed of becoming a doctor; she took great interest in studying the human body.

Her body was changing as well. She could feel it at that very moment – cramps in the stomach. All the girls in her class were already accustomed to the change, but she was yet to get her first period. She tried to focus on the diagram of the alveolar sac on the board, but the cramps got worse. Grabbing the sanitary napkin her mother had packed in her school bag for emergencies, Anahita rushed to the washroom. She wished Mehr was around; it would have been a lot easier if her best friend was there to support her.

A few minutes later, Anahita emerged from the bathroom, relieved. It was a false alarm! Suddenly, Anahita heard a girl's scream. It came from her classroom, and she recognized it instantly – Mehr. At the sound of a second scream, Anahita sprinted back to the class.

What she saw froze the blood in her veins.

15

Present Day
Midnight, Paradise Heights

ANAHITA WOKE FROM SLEEP, DISTURBED BY THE MEMORY that had crept into her dreams. Beads of sweat trickled down the backside of her neck like drops of rain over the glass surface of the balcony door. Seeing Mehr at the party had sent her subconsciously tumbling down memory lanes. Her sleepy eyes surveyed the misty darkness that had settled inside the bedroom. The place at present, just like Mehr from the party, had changed in appearance, but the sound of raindrops hitting the walls outside were exactly as they were in her dream. Scientists claim dreams do not actually have any sound. However, in the REM stage of sleep, the brain picks up the noises occurring outside the body, and makes it a part of the dream. The sound heard in the dream is thus incorporated from reality, in a manner that makes sense to the subconscious. In some cases, the sound outside can influence the dream.

Next to Anahita, Varun slept peacefully. Through the glass door, a bolt of lightning flashed and lit up the room for a moment. The sound followed instantly. Anahita stood up to draw the curtain, or the lightning would not let her sleep. Her blanket slid off her body and fell to the floor as she meandered to the door. Thoughts about seeing Mehr at the party and her dream filled Anahita's mind, but she tried her best to ignore them. She clenched the curtain's fabric with her right hand and was about to pull it when there was another flash. In that moment, as light illuminated everything, Anahita saw a woman in a fluttering maroon dress, drenched in the rain, standing outside the window, looking at her piercingly. Anahita shrieked in horror and recoiled in shock, clutching the curtain as she fell on the floor. The fabric ripped off and fell over her face. Everything went black.

'Anahita? Anahita?' The thud of his wife's fall had woken Varun up. Anxiously, he rushed over to see Anahita on the floor, the curtain over her head. He removed it and turned her around. 'What happened? What are you doing on the floor? Did you hurt yourself?'

Anahita came to her senses, trying to fathom what happened a moment ago. The fiery face of the woman at the glass door appeared in her mind.

'Anahita?'

'Varun ...' Anahita finally spoke, turning her head towards the glass door that led to the balcony. She raised her left hand like a zombie and pointed at the door. 'There was someone out there ... a woman.'

'What? What are you saying? A woman? How is that even possible?'

'There was someone. She looked so pale ... almost white!'

Varun got up and went outside to check in the rain. There was nobody. He was wet when he came inside. Irritated, he looked at Anahita and said, 'There is no one outside. No one can climb to the seventh floor of this building in this rain unless she is some superwoman or a ghost.'

Anahita shivered. *Confusion.* Too many thoughts, too many noises in her head.

Varun sighed. He took pity at his wife's condition and changed his tone. 'Anahita, there was no one. It was just a dream. Maybe you saw your own reflection.' He helped her up from the floor and held her close to his wet body. 'Maybe you should speak to Dr Malhotra about changing your medication. Lately, it hasn't been effective.'

Anahita nodded, not telling Varun that she had stopped taking her medication entirely, afraid that it might harm her child.

'I will change,' Varun said, looking at this wet pyjamas. 'You take your medicine and try to sleep.'

On the way out, Varun switched on the night lamp. Anahita did not dare to look out the glass door. She closed her eyes tightly, like Mehr had told her years ago. *Breathe in, breathe out, let it go!*

16

8 August 2019, Thursday
Crawford Market

ANOTHER GLOOMY DAY IN THE WETTEST TIME OF THE year. The rain subsided at four in the morning, but the grey clouds brazenly engulfed the noon sky. Keshav pressed his foot on the accelerator, making his way swiftly through the gaps in the traffic. He chewed on a betel leaf while humming a local song that played on the radio. Anahita was lost in thought about the two women she saw last night – one warm and familiar, one strange and frightening. She had decided long back that she would never see Mehr again; they had parted ways in the most dramatic way possible, and that happened not once but twice in her life; first in 2005 when they were in ninth grade and then again in 2010 during Anahita's brief stay in Mumbai.

Anahita knew Mehr lived in Mumbai, and that there was a one in a million chance of bumping into an ex-friend. It could have happened in a crowded mall or a market, where Anahita could change her path to skip the awkward moment. But it happened at a party of a few hundred people soon after she went through an episode of frenzy. The thought came back to her, and she started wondering if that woman who appeared outside the glass door was a figment of her imagination based on her meeting with Mehr. *Yes, she resembled her. I am sure she looked like Mehr.* Anahita was trying to convince herself but without great luck.

It left her with little choice but to speak with Dr Malhotra. Her husband did not listen to her anymore. He was getting tired of her endless issues. He did not have time or patience for such matters. Earlier in the morning, Varun kissed her on the forehead, and on his way out, he had advised her to fix an appointment with Dr Malhotra over Skype. All Anahita wanted was for someone to hear her out. Every time she visited Dr Malhotra, she felt like a patient, even though they used a fancy term – client. She wondered if Keshav could be a good listener, but then she heard him cuss at a beggar at a crossing. She decided against it.

Keshav knew Mumbai well, and he was taking her to the cloth market in the old town. Crawford Market, an undetachable part of Mumbai's history, was situated opposite Mumbai Police's headquarters, less than a mile from the grand old VT (CST) Station. The market has buildings that flaunt a Norman style of architecture; one gets a feeling that the buildings have come straight out of a Dickens story. He pulled over the car at the side of the crowded road in front of the police headquarters.

'Madam, we have arrived,' the driver announced.

Anahita came out of her thoughts and looked at the old buildings and cramped street. 'Is this Crawford Market?'

'Mahatma Jyotiba Phule Market, madam,' Keshav corrected Anahita. 'The old name was Crawford. I will park the car somewhere close by. Once you finish, call me. I hope you have my number.'

'Yes, Varun gave it to me in the morning.'

'I do not have your number, madam. Please give me a missed call.' The driver kept his eye fixed on Anahita in the rear-view mirror, as she got out of the car.

Noticing zero signal bars on her phone's screen, Anahita said, 'I will give you a missed call in some time. My sim does not seem to pick up any network here. It is a Delhi number, you know. Just so that you can recognize, my number ends with 2611.'

'Okay, madam, but don't forget to call when you are about to leave. It is very difficult to move a car in this crowded place. I will park at Flora.'

'I understand, Keshav. You can share your location with me. I will find you,' Anahita said.

'I don't trust your Delhi sim card.' Keshav giggled as if he had cracked a joke. Anahita had heard from a friend of hers that some Mumbaikars never missed a chance to crack a joke or two about Delhiwallahs. She forced a smile and left.

17

CRAWFORD MARKET MIGHT BE THE BEATING HEART OF Mumbai, but the rains left the roads muddy and waterlogged. The stench of drainage overwhelmed the petrichor that blended with the occasional aroma of *atar*. Anahita Anand wasn't a big fan of shopping and always avoided crowded places. Crowds made her anxious and somebody would always accompany her every time she had to go shopping – her mother, cousin or husband. A couple of weeks before leaving Delhi, she had read a book on overcoming anxiety that made a deep impact on her psyche. She let go of her fears and started travelling alone in buses. She would skip appointments with Dr Malhotra and go to crowded places without her husband. Varun welcomed the change in his wife's attitude, tired of her constant anxiety and fears. Varun also did not like the idea of depending on beta-blockers. In fact, it was Varun who gifted her a pile of self-help books, hoping that one of them might impact her positively, and it certainly had! But more than anything, Varun wished that his wife would get over her genophobia. She could only have sex with him when she was drunk, and at first, Varun did not mind. However, once she stopped drinking about five weeks ago, their sex life became non-existent and things devolved – a genophobic wife and a desperate husband.

As Anahita walked into one store, she noticed vivid varieties of curtains. She wanted blue silk or velvet curtains, to complement the red of the walls in the living room. As for the ones in the bedroom, she wanted something softer. The shop had over a dozen underaged sales boys tending to customers. After spending an hour, she had what she wanted. Anahita took her haul to the billing counter and waited for the old man with a long beard to tend her exact change. The sales boy had packed her curtains in a big cloth bag and handed it over to her with a courteous smile. Anahita smiled back and handed out a fifty-rupee note without hesitation. Reluctant at first, the boy happily accepted the tip and went back to work.

Anahita came out on the street; the stench pierced into her nose and replaced the charming smell of moist fabric with that of sewage. Her next destination was Gulshan Café, the famous Irani restaurant, where she hoped to sip on a cup of Irani chai and have a Shawarma roll. She had read excellent reviews online while she was at the curtain shop. The thought of roasted meat and spicy gravy inside *khuboos* stimulated her taste buds. The reviews mentioned that the restaurant was very clean, and that gave her some relief. As she waddled through the sea of uncaring customers and loud shopkeepers, for a moment, she felt that old feeling of being followed. Anxiety had defeated lessons learned from the self-help book.

When Anahita turned, she noticed a hundred people in as many square feet. Who could it be? She was about to walk away when she bumped into a man with a crooked back, about fifty. He had blisters all over his face and his skin was withered like a worn-out leather sole. The grey eyes looked lifeless, just like the woman Anahita had seen at the glass door. She flinched and stumbled backwards, almost falling down, but someone from behind steadied her.

'*Kaaye madam, dekh ke chalne ka na!*'

Anahita looked at the hunchback. He was still there, a battered tin bowl in his weathered hands. '*Allah ke naam pe de de …* '

Anahita felt sorry for him. She had another fifty in her purse and she gave it to him. He smiled at the generosity – he was used to coins, if anything. Anahita resumed her walk towards her destination. On the way, she crossed an old apartment complex called Sheila Cooperative Society. She read the rusty board with a vague sense of recognition.

Was I here before? Is it possible? Or am I just imagining things again. Once more, she felt eyes on her. When she turned, she saw that it was the beggar, his gaze almost piercing her skin. A sharp noise rang in her ears, and she could hear nothing else. Her head felt heavy, and as she looked around, the surrounding faces were all blurry. Among them, a familiar face passed by – a girl. Was it Mehr?

The pungent smell from the drainage seeped in through her nose; *bad air* filled her lungs. The faces blurred further into a string of jagged lines and things started to lose colour, until all of it turned to black.

18

7E, Paradise Heights

WHEN SHE OPENED HER EYES, ANAHITA WAS INSIDE her bedroom. *What happened? I was just in the market … Was it all my imagination, a dream?* She noticed she was wearing the same black top that she had worn to the market. *Was it really a dream? Wasn't I wearing the same clothes?* She noticed mud stains on the jeans.

Shh. Breathe in. Breathe out. Everything is under control.

Anahita tried to calm herself down as she sat up on the bed. Her glance fell on the brand-new white curtain dangling from the rod ahead of the glass door.

Who fixed the curtain rod? Wasn't this the curtain that I had bought?

Anahita tiptoed towards the glass door in disbelief. With shivering hands, she examined the netted fabric. It felt exactly like the one she had bought … *or dreamt she had bought.* From where she stood, she could see the greyish sky through the

86

glass door. That was where she had seen the apparition a night ago.

'Who were you, woman? Why were you trying to scare me?' Anahita asked in frustration. She let go of the curtain and was about to go to the bathroom when she heard clinking sounds from the kitchen.

'Who is there?' Anahita called out, hurrying towards the sound. There was a ceramic vase lying on the table in the bedroom – something she had brought from her old house. She picked it up cautiously and continued to the kitchen. Every step she took disturbed the stale air inside the house. She clutched on to the vase tightly, ready to whack the potential intruder, her heart racing. The kitchen door opened and Anahita's hand rose, ready to strike the figure walking out. But when she saw who it was, her fingers went numb and she dropped the vase on the floor, shattering it into pieces.

It was Mehr.

19

<div align="center">~~~</div>

MNP Headquarters

Bhau met all of Varun's demands and lavishly. A spacious working space on the third floor of the building, large enough for about ten people. A private cabin for Varun. He had hired four new resources from Mumbai in his team and kept five remote resources from his original team that worked with him during the Delhi elections. The rest of his staff, which included content writers, communication executives, and social media managers, worked from Tinsel's Gurugram office. Bhau even made Rekha Dutt, the girl at the reception, Varun's personal assistant – a promotion for Rekha. Somebody else took over her job at the reception. Varun hoped she would return the favour someday.

Sitting in his cabin, Varun summoned Rekha. In seconds, she walked in, wearing a beige-coloured top that kissed her skin.

'Everyone settled?' he asked.

'I believe so, Varun.' She held an open notepad in her hand.

'Great. How about you? Are you ready to work with me? It is going to be a fun ride for you and me … hopefully.'

She returned his smile. 'I am looking forward to the *ride*.'

'Well, the *ride* starts with a *toolkit*.' Varun switched to a commanding tone. 'I want you to get me a list of all environmental activists based out of Mumbai – the local ones. I also need to know their political affiliations and engagement metrics on social media, especially on Twitter. If the activist is loyal to the ruling party, then I don't want that person on the list. Do you get me?'

'Yes, Varun.' She noted them down in her notepad.

'Also, a list of social media influencers with verified profiles who are politically neutral or inclined towards Bhau's party.'

'When do you need these?'

'Now.'

'Of course! Anything else?'

'That will do for now.'

'All right!' Rekha smiled. She closed her notepad and walked towards the door.

'And Rekha …'

She stopped at the door. 'Yes?'

'Fix me an appointment with all the news agencies that are aligned with MNP. I need all appointments to be scheduled before the end of this week – regional news channels first, then national television, then newspapers and online news portals.'

'Right!'

'Thanks, Rekha.'

Varun knew he had a herculean task ahead of him, but he was always ready with a plan. He had to pitch as the future leader of the state a brat who could not even lead his own life properly. Plus unlike in Delhi, the ruling party here wasn't facing any anti-incumbency at all. In fact, the major media outlets were projecting a clean sweep for them. Bhau was aware of this, and that was why he wanted to introduce his nephew. Because if they lost the elections, that would make it two terms in a row without MNP being in power. It would diminish Bhau's political clout, and he might no longer be able to launch his nephew five years later, when he himself would likely be struggling. After all, people had already started rejecting dynasty politics. If his nephew had any chance to survive, then this was it. So Bhau roped in Varun, who had changed the shape of Delhi's political scenario, hopeful that he would do the same to Bhau's MNP in Maharashtra. Varun understood this, and he was confident that he would be able to repeat his success in Mumbai as well. His confidence was rewarded with an email from one of his trusted informants telling him about the biggest newsbreak of the year, which was sure to bring down the ruling party and get Bhau on top again.

It was only a matter of time ... and some *prime* time.

20

A few minutes later

ANAHITA TUGGED MEEKLY AT THE TOWER BOLT. IT seemed stuck. Mehr came forward.

'Wait, let me … ' Mehr pulled the latch with brute force and it came open. The women stepped outside. 'Wow! What a spectacular view,' Mehr said, noting the cars and BEST buses on the wet road right before looking around at the isolated patch of green estate. She asked, 'You guys must shell out a lot of money for this apartment.'

'Not really.' Anahita stretched her arms. She felt like she had just woken from a long sleep, no headache or blocked nose. As if the part of her that gave pain separated itself from her. She felt fine, as if she had never fainted, or maybe it was because she was in the presence of someone she knew.

'Then?' Mehr asked, confused.

'Well, this house belongs to the politician, Deshmukh.'

'Bhau,' Mehr corrected. 'Oh yes, your husband works for him. You told me last night. What does he do?' Mehr knew nothing about Anahita's married life.

'He runs a start-up called Tinsel. It looks after election PR. Right now, he is looking after Deshmukh's party.' Anahita revealed. She noticed something unusual about Mehr. She looked different from the night before. Maybe it was the maroon frames of her eyeglasses; Mehr wasn't wearing them the previous night. Maybe it was Mehr's hairstyle. Far away, a bus honked.

'How did it happen?' Mehr asked, her voice getting heavier with unspoken grief.

Anahita looked away from her friend and said, 'My mom has known Varun since he was a teenager. He was a family friend's son who happened to have a crush on me. We went out for a while. It felt good to have someone … again. He proposed.'

'Wait … your mother didn't stop you from going out with a boy and all?'

'Actually, it was she who encouraged me to go out with Varun. She thought he was a brilliant prospect. You can say she kind of pushed me into saying yes … indirectly.'

'Of course, that woman is so pushy.'

'She is not a bad person, Mehr, it is just …'

'It is just what, Anahita?'

Anahita turned towards Mehr. 'She is not like *us*.'

'Us?' Mehr sighed. 'It is you and *only you*. I do not exist, Anahita. I do not exist. Isn't that how it ended nine years ago?'

'Please, Mehr, I don't want to think about all that. I am just thrilled to see you after so many years.'

'You didn't seem so thrilled last night though, at the party.'

'I was just … shocked. It took some time to sink in. Besides, Varun was there, and I felt uncomfortable with the two of you together in one frame.'

'The past and present colliding for you, wasn't it?'

Anahita did not reply.

'Are you happy?' Mehr asked.

'I know I cannot keep my husband happy. I just can't … after what happened in school, I just can't let anyone … You don't know, Mehr. I might breathe in the present, but my mind keeps going back and forth. Nobody can understand what I am going through. It is like hell in here.' Anahita slammed her palm on her forehead.

'All right, okay … Calm down. Breathe in, breathe out,' Mehr said embracing her friend, 'things will be fine. I am here for you. I don't know if you believe in destiny … I don't … but the fact that you are in this city, and that you fainted in the middle of a market in the afternoon and me being there just makes me wonder if there is a higher power controlling us like pawns and pieces in this game of existence. I could have gone there tomorrow, but I went today. As if I had to go to bring you home. And thanks to your husband,' Mehr changed her tone to a lighter one, 'for giving me your address at the party.' Mehr laughed and Anahita chuckled between sobs. 'Now cheer up, Anahita.'

'You look younger today,' Anahita said finally.

'No makeup!'

Anahita came out of the embrace. She loved the warmth of Mehr's arms. It felt like the good old days, the years when she had no one else to go to. She remembered all those moments in life shared with Mehr. At that moment, Anahita was going through a terrible dilemma. *Perhaps it is indeed destiny that has brought Mehr back into my life*. Anahita gathered courage to divulge her secret. 'Mehr …'

'Yes, Anahita.'

'I am pregnant!'

'What? Is it … his?'

'Yes! Obviously!'

'Then why do you look so … weary?'

Silence followed. Anahita's eyes twitched.

'Wait. He doesn't know it yet, does he?'

'It is complicated. Besides, he says he is not ready for a child. If he comes to know that I am pregnant, and the way I got him to do this … then he will …' Anahita's eyes filled with tears.

Mehr grabbed her head and placed it back on her shoulder. She patted Anahita's back like a mother consoles a daughter in pain. Anahita continued. 'I want to have this baby. I can't tell you how lonely I feel nowadays. It is just that I know I cannot raise a baby on my own … in my condition. I need Varun to be completely on my side, or …'

'Shh … calm down. Anahita, you don't always get what you want. Sometimes you must let one thing go to get another one. You may have to choose what is more important.'

Anahita lifted her head. 'I can't …'

'You can! You have done it in the past. You might have to do it again. Cruel as it may be … *choose*. Let go of things that are holding you back, making you unhappy. And make place for the right things. You cannot always be at other people's mercy; back then it was your mother and now …'

The doorbell rang. Anahita wiped her tears and quickly went inside. From the balcony, Mehr looked through the glass door as her old friend disappeared inside the house.

21

⌇

AFTER DROPPING ANAHITA AT CRAWFORD MARKET, Keshav parked the car in front of his friend's inn on the Lokmanya Tilak Marg. He spent some time with his friend, talking about politics and the usual stuff. It was after they had a cup of tea and snacks that the driver realized he had not heard from the woman for over two hours. He pulled out his phone and checked if she had dropped any missed calls – none! He cursed himself for not taking her number before the woman went off. He could not think of calling anyone from the party office because it would leak the information to Bhau that he could not perform his assigned duty. That would make a poor impression on Bhau, and a loyal party worker would not want that taint. People like Keshav lived and died to be in the good books of their all-powerful leaders!

Keshav looked around in Crawford Market but could not find Anahita anywhere. Then, finally, he heard from someone that a woman matching the description had fainted near the Masjid gully. But no one knew what happened to her afterwards; one person said that she had only tripped, another said she had fainted and was carried away. Keshav decided to check the apartment before starting a search party.

That is how he had arrived outside 7E. The guard was absent and Keshav stood in anticipation after ringing the doorbell, pulse racing, until he heard the metallic sound of the bolt clinking against the hinge. The door opened and Mrs Anand stood there, looking perfectly fine; only her eyes looked heavy, as if she had wept moments ago.

'Madam!' Keshav exclaimed in relief. 'You are back! Why didn't you give me a missed call?' Words spurted out of his mouth like bubbles on the surface of boiling water.

'I am so sorry. I fainted in the market. Luckily, my friend who was there spotted me in time and brought me back.'

'Your friend?' Keshav tried to peep in from where he stood.

'Yes.'

'Are you all right now?' He asked, scanning her face and arms for scratches or wounds.

'Touch-wood, I am.' Anahita stroked the surface of the door with her hand.

'Okay,' he said, stepping back. 'Is there anything you need? Medicine? Groceries?'

'Nothing right now. I will let you know. Thank you.'

The driver appeared confused. He pulled out his phone from the back pocket of his pants and said, 'Can you please give me your phone number? I will note down and save it in my phone.'

'Yes.'

Anahita dictated her number to the driver. The driver saved it as *Anahita Madam* and returned the phone to his pocket. He smiled and left. As he walked towards the elevator, he heard Anahita speak to someone.

'Are you leaving too?'

'Yes, I … I have … stuff to do. I will catch up with you later.' The voice of another woman.

'Bye, Mehr.'

'Take care.'

Keshav deduced that this must be the friend who had found his madam at the market. As he pressed the elevator button, he heard the door of 7E shutting behind him. Keshav stepped inside the elevator and looked out, expecting Anahita's friend to enter any second. But the floor was empty; no one approached the elevator. He heard the sound of footsteps going down the stairs.

'These urban women, so obsessed with fitness. I can't think of taking seven flights of stairs,' Keshav mumbled. Then he remembered that Anahita too had not stepped inside the elevator a few days back when he had brought her to see the apartment. Maybe all her friends were like her – afraid. The thought lingered in his mind only for a moment and then faded away. Keshav was just glad his madam was safe. *At least Bhau will not be disappointed.*

22

MEHR'S DEPARTURE LEFT THE APARTMENT DESERTED again. Anahita wanted to lie down and read a book. She picked one from the shelf in the study room. She had been inside all the other rooms of the apartment. A lot of the stuff in that apartment had been untouched for ages; the library was one of those. That day, the room felt warmer than the rest of the house. She opened the window, letting in a wave of fresh monsoon air.

Déjà vu – something reminded her of the bookshelf she had while growing up in her Gurugram home. She browsed through the rack at eye-level; full of classics and most of the volumes imported before 1950. She caught hold of Oscar Wilde's *The Picture of Dorian Gray* – the story of a man's never-ending tryst with his desires. It was one of her favourites. She first read it in ninth standard, just days before that dreaded eighth day of August in 2005. Still slave to the trauma, Anahita pushed the book back to the shelf. The upper rack had a few bound scripts, a few manuscripts without cover, and many tattered books on death: *Staring Into The Endless Depth; Life After Death; Is It The End?; What Is It Like To Be*

Dead?; Through The Gates Of Death; Garudapurana: The Book Of Forbidden Knowledge; The Black Arts; All Of Them Witches; The Parsi Way Of Life; Afterlife In Islam; Life After Life; Laws Of The Spirit World. At the far end, there stood a book with a thick brown cover – some sort of journal.

Anahita skipped everything else and reached out for it. She wiped the dust with the side of her palm and tried to decipher the bold letters on the cover. She could not read it. They looked like curved lines arranged in a vaguely recognizable pattern. She felt a strange mix of curiosity and familiarity. Something felt off, but the intrigue was far more compelling. Anahita opened the book; the pages were yellow with age, almost tearing at the edges.

The first page was blank. Like any bookworm would do, Anahita moved her face closer to the surface and sniffed it; the scent of old paper rushed inside. She coughed, then flipped the page. A breeze moved in from the window, causing a pane to bang against the sill. Anahita turned to the window briefly, distracted by the noise. Then she turned back to look at the open book. Something was written on the second page in blue ink. Maybe a name? But it was in a script alien to Anahita. She rubbed her index finger over the name, feeling the uneven hardness of the paper's surface. When Anahita removed her finger from the page, she noticed that the shadow of a finger remained over it. Instinctively, she turned around. A chill ran down her spine as she watched a silhouetted figure disappear outside the window. She rushed to the window and looked out – nothing. Then, she heard the flapping of wings above her. When she looked up, she caught sight of a gigantic bird with a long neck soaring into the grey sky.

A vulture? She tried to focus on the flying creature. Before she could figure it out, a lightning bolt struck in the sky, and she lost track of the bird. Another bolt of lightning flashed in the sky. Anahita looked away, blinded by the blaze, and in that moment, she noticed a woman staring at her from the apartment's main gate – a woman in a maroon dress.

It was the woman she had seen in her balcony the other night.

23

ANAHITA SCURRIED ALONG THE BRICK-LAID PATH THAT led to the main gate, like a rat hit by a fit of frenzy. Her eyes scanned every inch of the surroundings, looking for any signs of the pale woman. The guard's cabin was vacant, as it had been ever since she had moved to that apartment.

How can they not have a guard if it is such a prime property? Isn't there an active resident's welfare association or something? Anahita wondered as she went looking inside the cabin. There were some old newspapers, a small CRT television from the late nineties and a soggy register to maintain entries. The forty-watt incandescent bulb on the ceiling looked ancient. Anahita checked the day's entry in the soggy register. To her surprise, the last entry was made at 11 a.m. There were no records of anyone entering or exiting the building after that.

Did Mehr not sign on the register because she was carrying me? Maybe the watchman helped her carry me upstairs and forgot to ask her to sign?

'Can I help you, madam?' An elderly male voice barked from behind in Hindi.

Instinctively, Anahita slammed the register shut and turned. The seventy-something watchman stood there in his blue uniform. His face had wrinkled into layers like a pug's cheeks. He was chewing on betel leaves.

'Oh, I am sorry. Are you the watchman?'

'Yes, can't you see me wearing this darned uniform?'

'I am Anahita Anand. I just moved into this apartment with my husband.'

'7E! Tenants?'

'Yes!'

'I know about you guys. Why were you looking inside my cabin?'

'My friend, she came over to see me.'

'So? Did she steal anything from your place?'

'What? No! I felt like there was someone down here staring at my window. Did you notice her? A lady with trimmed hair.'

'Was it your friend?'

'No.'

'Listen, many people come here every day. It is beyond my pay grade to remember each one, especially when it is raining twenty-four seven. You know what I am saying?'

'I didn't mean to offend you.' Anahita felt genuinely apologetic. 'Oh, I wanted to ask. How come there is no entry on the register for my friend who just visited me? She was with me in my apartment. Even my driver had come afterwards, but neither of them show up in your register.'

'Oh! So, is that the problem? The old watchman is not doing his duties properly? Why don't you complain to the resident's association?'

'You don't have to be so rude, *bhaiyya*.'

'The rich people here have installed a camera,' he said and pointed towards the CCTV unit clinging under the beams of the first building block. 'When you can see it, why bother checking the register?'

'Can you show me the footage?'

'No!'

'No?'

'Lightning damaged the camera last night,' the old watchman said casually. 'Now go back to your house. Stop bothering me.' He dismissed her and stepped inside his cabin. He sat on his wooden chair and looked away.

Anahita was annoyed with the watchman's behaviour, but she was also too tired to take the stairs. *How do I take the elevator?* She turned to the watchman once more, who had now picked up a newspaper. 'Can you please accompany me to my apartment? I am not comfortable travelling in the elevator by myself.'

Without taking his eyes off the newspaper, the watchman replied, 'Why don't you wait outside for some time, madam? I am sure that someone will come along.'

Anahita regretted asking for his help. Quietly, she returned to her block and sat down on one of the leather cushioned sofas, waiting. If no one showed up, she would call Keshav. That was her plan. Only a severe claustrophobe like her would go to such lengths. After waiting for a few minutes, Anahita saw a woman – about as old as Anahita's mother – approach the building and walk towards the elevator. Anahita rushed behind her and entered before the doors could close, catching the elderly woman by surprise.

'I am so sorry for coming in like this … I'm claustrophobic.'

'Is that why you were waiting in the reception?' The woman asked, each word uttered with the grace of a sophisticated person.

'I requested the watchman, but he did not seem to care much for residents.'

'Oh, Rattan, that old bastard is like that. He has gone through a lot in recent years and has become irate with age. We usually ignore him; you should too. After his time, I hope they will hire someone younger.' The woman pressed on the button that read seven on the board.

'You stay on the seventh floor as well?' Anahita asked, a spark of joy gently lighting up her face.

'7D.'

'I am Anahita, Anahita Anand. 7E.'

The information cast a shadow on the woman's face. Covering up, she said, 'Rosemary … I'm Rosemary.'

The elevator doors closed and it started its ascension.

'This is such a beautiful building,' Anahita exclaimed.

'Isn't it? We were one of the first families to move when they constructed it back in 1996. There were not many high-rise buildings to challenge its look and feel back then. Paradise Heights was a gem for the elite,' Rosemary spoke, her eyes glistening at the thought of a bygone era.

'But why does it look so empty now? I hardly see any residents around.'

'Many have moved out; many died. It is an old building with its own history. Time moves differently in such places, young lady. It is older than you, I am guessing.'

'I am sure it is.'

The elevator stopped and the doors parted. They came out into the passage. 'Thank you so much, Rosemary!' Anahita said.

'There is no need for that, Anahita. You should come to me if you need anything at all,' the elder woman offered gracefully. 'Besides, you are very brave to spend time alone in 7E.'

'Why do you say that?'

'I assumed you knew about the building and its history, especially since 7E was at the heart of the haunting.' Rosemary noticed the blank expression on the young tenant's face. 'Do you live by yourself?'

'No, I live with my husband.'

'I see. You and your husband should discuss it with the agent or the landlord. You did not hear this from me.' The old woman gently squeezed Anahita's hand. 'Now, I must take your leave. It is time for my medicines.' Rosemary turned and moved towards her door, about a hundred meters from Anahita's apartment.

'Of course! See you.'

'I hope so!' Rosemary whispered to herself as she disappeared into the passage that led to 7D.

Anahita went inside her apartment, this time with a heavy feeling in her gut. As she shut the door behind her, she felt like the entire house was crumbling inside a ball of vacuum. It was time to take that pill, but she did not want to consume anything that might harm the baby growing inside her. But stress wasn't good for the baby either. Maybe it was time to talk to someone. The phone inside her pocket rang as if it understood its owner's dilemma. Anahita checked the screen; it was Dr Malhotra.

24

Varun arrived home late in the night, tired from his meetings during the day. Anahita served him dal-chawal. Anahita knew it didn't taste good, but her husband hardly cared for such stuff anymore. He had too much going on inside his head and just needed food to keep his body up and running; taste did not matter. Whenever he felt like his taste buds needed something refreshing, he would dine out with his colleagues or secretaries. Nevertheless, Anahita prepared the food and did daily chores. She was used to the routine. Her mother had trained her to be a *good* wife.

Varun finished his dinner quietly and went off to bed without talking much. When Anahita came to the bedroom, he was shooting text messages and emails to people.

'Do you need anything, dear?' Anahita asked as she placed the bottle of warm water near the bedside table.

'Nope,' Varun said, without looking at his wife.

'All right. I am going to sleep then.'

Varun continued typing and swiping on the cellular phone. An awkward silence took over the bedroom, just like all other nights. She had crossed the first trimester, but she could not tell her husband. Before she got pregnant, she could at least get drunk and engage with her husband in some capacity. She felt responsible for the relationship that was crumbling like the last piece of the stale cake from their first marriage anniversary, the only time Anahita felt that they truly loved each other.

Anahita had spoken about it with Dr Malhotra in the evening when she had called. The psychiatrist suggested that she break the shell before it rotted. Paranoia was taking over Anahita's sanity. She feared that if she took any medication to suppress her depressing thoughts or delusions it would harm the baby growing inside her. She could not tell Varun because he might also force her to abort, and she did not want that at any cost. When Anahita confided about the pale woman at the glass door, Dr Malhotra prescribed her a milder anti-depressant. She also advised her to talk about it with her husband, to help her feel better.

Anahita thought she would give it a try. 'Varun?'

'Yes?'

'How was your day?'

'Not great. All these new people and places. It will take time to settle down, and I hardly have time, you know. What about you? I am glad you got some decent looking curtains.'

'I … I thought you would like them.'

'How did you place the rod back on the wall? Did Keshav help?'

The curtain stood at over eight feet. Anahita had wondered too, because she could remember nothing at all. She said what seemed to be the only reasonable explanation. 'I … I managed with the help of a friend. Mehr.'

'Mehr?' Varun kept the phone on the table and turned towards Anahita. 'Your friend came home?'

'Yes!'

'Must be a very close one.'

'She was.'

'And gorgeous too.'

She is not your type, Varun, Anahita said in her mind as she smiled at her husband.

Now that Varun was finally looking at her, Anahita decided to broach the topic. 'Varun, do you find anything strange about this house?'

'What?'

'I know you did not believe me when I said I saw a woman in the balcony. But doesn't something feel creepy about this place?'

'I think it is a beautiful apartment. A gated society. Very safe.'

'But that watchman is weird.'

'If you want, I can ask Keshav to arrange a maid or someone to stay with you at home …'

'No, that's okay. I can manage.'

'Okay, good!' He picked up his phone again. 'How was your e-session with Dr Malhotra?'

'It was okay. She asked me to schedule an appointment with a …' Anahita almost spilled it. She paused.

'With?'

'With a yoga instructor or someone who can help with mindfulness meditation.' Anahita lied, her fingers fidgeting. *Tell him about the pregnancy! Tell him Malhotra wanted you to schedule an appointment with a gynae!*

'All right! Anything else you want to talk about?'

Anahita could see the subtle look of annoyance in Varun's eyes. 'No … nothing.'

Anahita wanted to tell him that the neighbour, Rosemary, told her that the building had a history. She wanted to tell him she would love to make love to him, but for that she would have to get drunk and take her old anti-depressant. But she could not do this, because she was pregnant with his child. Anahita wanted to tell her husband that she wouldn't get rid of the baby even if he threatened to leave her. She wanted to tell him that Mehr was not just an old friend. Anahita wanted to tell him a lot of things, but she suppressed everything in her mind, just like she had done every night for the last three months.

'Okay, I have to finish going through these reports and campaign plans. So, don't wait for me.'

'Goodnight, dear.'

'Goodnight!'

Anahita turned away and tried to sleep, but five minutes later, she got up from the bed and went to check the glass door. There was nobody outside. She pulled the curtain so that it left no gap for any kind of peek-a-boos. Varun was still on the phone. Anahita came back to the bed, picked up her phone and searched for Mehr on Instagram. She clicked on the first profile that appeared; it was her friend's. Anahita pressed on *message* and in the screen that opened, she typed:

Did not expect to bump into you so quickly. Thanks for not ignoring me. I thought you would not even talk to me after the way it ended.

Anahita paused, and added:

Sorry, forgot to exchange phone numbers. Ping me.

She expected a reply from her friend, but she also feared that she might choose not to. So she locked the phone, placed it near her head and closed her eyes. Fifteen minutes later, she was lost in a dream from the past.

---

13 August 2005, Saturday
Good Shepherd Convent, Gurgaon

All students in the tenth and ninth grade knew that Christopher and Mehr were dating. Christopher's friends had put pressure on the boy, who had a reputation to maintain. They kept asking him every day if he had done it yet. He kept saying no to them, but he feared they would soon tag him as a loser who could not pop his cherry despite having a hot girlfriend. Initially, he tried to woo Anahita, but she was not the girl who would mingle with boys. She was the teacher's pet. It was during his struggle with Anahita that he got closer to Mehr, and eventually, the tomboy fell for the charmer. Anahita and Mehr drifted apart like the vertices of a line, though she would say nothing about it to her friend.

Christopher had touched Mehr a few times and even made out with her, but eventually, he wanted to go further. The first day after the school reopened, he came only because he knew he would catch Mehr alone during the zero period. The entire floor was empty, and he made sure that the coast was clear. First, he promised Mehr that he would get her a cigarette after school. That promise got Mehr excited; it would be her first time trying one. She had her alibi ready: group study at Anahita's place.

Christopher and Mehr snuck back inside their classroom, thinking that everybody had left. He locked the door. They started making out. Mehr did that thing with her tongue that boys loved, but took forever to perfect. Christopher squeezed her breasts, and as she let out a sigh, his right hand wriggled under her skirt, tickling her thigh. She slapped his hand. She did not like that. 'Not yet,' she said, but he was desperate. This was the best chance he had. He tried to push her on to the desk and climb on to her, but she slipped out from under him.

'What the hell are you trying to do? I said no!'

'Why? Don't you love me?'

'Love? Well, I like you. But I need more time to …'

'Like? What the hell! If you only *like* me then why did you let me kiss you?'

'Coz I like you.'

'Do you kiss all the boys that you *like*?' He asked accusingly. 'You do what you want when you want it, right? You feel like kissing, you will kiss me. You feel like fucking, you will fuck me or whoever. Is it like that?'

'This is so typical!'

'You know what? I also *like* you. And I want to fuck you … now!'

'No.'

'Why no?'

'Because I said so, asshole!' Mehr turned angrily and walked towards the door.

Christopher pounced on her and they both went crashing down on the floor. The fall injured Mehr's hip. As she screamed in pain, Christopher climbed over her. A struggle ensued, and she finally managed to kick him right in the groin. He recoiled. With difficulty, Mehr rose from the floor and unbolted the door, but before she could escape, he caught hold of her. He grabbed her by the neck and tossed her towards the blackboard. When her back hit the board's surface, it smudged off the diagram of the respiratory system. The impact broke a bone somewhere and made her shriek again. She crumpled to the floor. She had lost the fight against her attacker.

Christopher unfastened his belt. He had asked his friends to guard the stairs from the floor below, so that no one entered their floor. Tears filled Mehr's eyes from pain and the helplessness. She remembered what her best friend, Anahita, had said about Christopher in the class.

I am telling you this boy is going to get you in trouble. Besides, I hate covering for you all the time.

Mehr wished she had listened to her. And then, the door opened with a bang, and in came Anahita – like a saviour. It took her a moment to realize what was going on. The horror on her face would ferment into a fit of fury in an instant.

25

9 August 2019, Friday
7E, Paradise Heights
3.45 a.m.

Anahita woke up gasping for air. It was pouring outside, with frequent bolts of lightning. Varun slept with his back towards her. Anahita noticed an unusual bloating in her tummy. A storm of gassy bubbles enveloped her oesophagus, and she felt an acerbic sugary taste in her throat. Rushing to the washroom, Anahita slouched over the commode and hurled. Once the ordeal was over and she had cleaned up, she stood looking at the mirror.

Is this your doing, Agastya? Ananya? These were the names she had chosen for her baby – Agastya for a boy, Ananya for a girl. *How tiny are you right now?* She thought, caressing her tummy. It felt warm and round, even though she did not remember this visible bump when she went to bed the night before. In fact, the bump looked larger than how it had been when she was vomiting.

But in a month's time your bump will start showing, what will you do then? Anahita recollected what her psychiatrist had said. She wondered if that was how the bump grew, suddenly, during a night's sleep. She had read how it was different for each woman – the bump, the sickness, the stress. She took a deep breath and blinked. A bubbling sensation. Little boils appeared on the bump until one of them exploded and a black slimy, tentacle waddled out of the crater, and then another one. Soon, there were eight of them squiggling and wiggling in an irregular pattern. The slimy thing looked like placenta lining above the creature's tentacles, and they grew in length until they rose towards Anahita's horror-stricken face. Before she knew, the tentacles pierced through her eyes, nostrils, ears, skull, and back.

⌇

3.45 a.m.

Anahita woke up sweating, her heart pounding against her chest. She checked her eyes, nose, ears, skull, and her back – one by one. All intact. Her stomach didn't show any baby bump. It was just a dream, a *nightmare*. Her shifting on the bed disturbed Varun's sleep, and he murmured something. But all Anahita could hear was the sound of her heartbeat and the rain pouring outside. She realized that the glass door was open, and the curtain fluttered in the cold monsoon breeze.

'Varun?' she whimpered. 'Varun?'

'Hmm … ?'

'Did you open the glass door?'

'No,' Varun replied, still half asleep.

'Then who did? I did not …'

Anahita's voice trailed off in shock when the silhouette of a vulture landed on the parapet of the balcony. She shook her husband to wake him up. 'Varun. Varun!' Inside, her heart was trying to break out of her chest, but she tried to maintain her calm on the outside.

Varun turned towards Anahita, frowning at her with sleepy eyes. 'What?'

With her gaze locked on the creature that had appeared outside, Anahita asked, 'Do you see that vulture on the parapet, Varun?'

'Vulture?' Varun squinted. At first everything appeared blurred, but then he focused. Rain poured inside from the open glass door. He looked at his wife, who was shivering in fear. 'Why did you open the door?'

'Please tell me you see it.'

'No … I don't see any vulture. Just rain.'

Varun had confirmed Anahita's suspicion. *I am hallucinating again.* Outside, lighting flashed. She closed her eyes tightly.

Breathe in. Breathe out.

'Varun, can you please get me a Cypene-10 tablet from the drawer? Please?' Anahita asked without opening her eyes.

26

———

Anahita took the new tablets reluctantly, and she slept peacefully till noon. When she woke up, the first thing she checked was her Instagram DMs. To her disappointment, Mehr had not even seen the message that Anahita had sent.

Varun had left for work. Anahita felt guilty because he had to take care of his own breakfast and the best he could do was cereal. Later in the day, she googled about Cypene-10 – the medication she was prescribed for hallucinations. The search results returned nothing positive for the expecting mother. She called up Dr Malhotra to reconsider her prescription.

'Doctor, I read on the internet that the medicine you prescribed might cause birth defects in my baby.' Anahita said.

'Yes, there is a probable risk,' the psychiatrist clarified, 'but it is *safer* than other drugs in the market.'

'But I don't want any harm to come to my baby, what do I do?'

The psychiatrist paused for a moment to consider her response. 'Anahita, you need to work on breath control.

Try yoga and meditation. I have recommended this many times before, but you never follow through. Sometimes such mindfulness meditation helps in calming down the mind. Take the medicine if and only if you have another visual hallucination.' The doctor paused for a moment and then said sternly, 'What about the gynae? Did you schedule an appointment?'

Guilt shadowed Anahita's face. Her silence answered Dr Malhotra's question.

'Anahita, I'd suggest you fix an appointment with a gynaecologist today itself, if possible, now!'

'I will do that … soon.'

Anahita slept shortly after that conversation. She did not have any dreams or hallucinations. At around 5 p.m., the doorbell rang, waking her up from her slumber. When she opened the door, she found Rosemary smiling at her, a plate of cake in her hand.

⸻

'My parents shifted to Gurugram when I was too young to remember,' Anahita told Rosemary as she took the last piece of the cake. 'But I did come to Mumbai occasionally. I used to do some modelling back in my college days. I wanted to move here, but my mother did not allow me.'

'I have been there once or twice. Gurugram. My niece was working in an MNC in DLF Phase-3. Quite a place,' Rosemary said, sitting gracefully on the old sofa in the living room. She kept glancing at the velvet fabric of the sofa. Right since she had arrived, Rosemary was behaving a bit weird. Initially, she did not want to step inside at all.

Anahita overlooked this and asked, 'How long have you been in Mumbai?'

'Long enough. I guess I will die here too. I think you have everything from all over the world here in Mumbai. Nowhere else in the world can you find such a charming city.'

'I agree.'

Rosemary swirled her finger over the velvet and said presciently, 'But it is a shrewd witch, you know, this city. Once you fall prey to its charm, it will wrap its tentacles around you. And before your mind can tell you to get out, it pulls you inside.'

Tentacles. Anahita thought about the dream she had the previous night. *Is this just a coincidence? Does she know something?* Anahita started sweating.

'Are you all right, dear?' Rosemary asked, looking at the panic-stricken face of her host.

Anahita smiled politely. 'I … I … just had some bad dreams last night. Started thinking about one of them, that's all.'

'Well, I am sure you won't be getting sugary dreams when you are living in this haunted house.' Rosemary's gaze shifted back to the velvet of the sofa. 'If I were you, I would not have moved in here.'

'Why do you say that? Last time too, you said something about this.' Anahita could not hold back her curiosity. 'And why do you keep looking at the sofa?'

'Nothing has changed in this house. It is exactly as it was when I came here last time. About two decades ago.'

'Did you know the previous owners?'

Rosemary shifted on the sofa uncomfortably. She clearly did not want to talk about what she knew, but somehow, she had taken a liking for the young girl from Gurugram.

'Look, Anahita. I am telling you this because I don't want you to get in any sort of trouble. I don't even know if you will believe me, but like I said, this house is haunted. The woman who lived here, she was not nice. Every time I go to the elevator, I cross this apartment, and I can feel an evil force trying to grab me.'

'What evil? The woman who lived here?' Anahita asked anxiously. 'Tell me, Rosemary!'

'It is the woman who *died* here.'

Anahita's face turned pale.

'She committed suicide. A few months after the suicide, the owners sold it off to someone. But the new owner never moved in, neither did they rent out the house. They had locked the house for all these years, everything left intact … until you moved in. However, I have heard sounds from inside. As if there was someone.'

The lamp that illuminated the room flickered a couple of times. Rosemary got up from her sofa and walked up to Anahita. The older woman kneeled in front of her and whispered, 'That woman … she did not even spare her daughter. Some say that she killed her daughter and ate her before killing herself. If I were you, I would not stay here for another night.' The lamp flickered again. Rosemary rose and started towards the main door. Anahita looked on as the guest opened the door and stepped outside.

'Get out while you still can. It won't be long before you also end up standing on the balcony's edge.'

Fear overwhelmed Anahita's anxious mind. She calmed herself down and got up to close the door. She was now certain that something was terribly wrong with the house they had decided to call home.

Anahita grabbed her phone and started searching for details pertaining to the house on the internet. She typed *suicide at 7E paradise heights,* but that did not return many results on Google. Most results were irrelevant, while a couple that seemed correct had broken URLs. She checked with another set of keywords: *haunted house paradise heights,* and this time she got a promising result that took her to the product page of an ecommerce website. The product was a book of horror short stories written by Hira Tejwani. The stories were true accounts of a paranormal investigator who had spent a night in the haunted places mentioned in the book. Apparently, one of the stories from the book was about a haunted apartment in Paradise Heights – 7E.

Anahita searched for the writer on Google and found his website. On the homepage, he claimed that he had driven away spirits by establishing contact with them through *scientific* means. Plenty of fans had commented on his paranormal investigation videos as well. There was a contact form at the bottom of the page. She left her phone number, asking the writer to contact her immediately. She did not know if the person would even have time to see her message, let alone call her back on the number.

Minutes later, her phone buzzed. She wondered if it was the writer. But it was something more pleasant – a message on Instagram from Mehr. To the message that Anahita had sent the previous night, Mehr had replied: *Likewise. Busy now. Have a couple of meetings. Will ping you later.*

The very thought of Mehr soothed Anahita's nerves. She forgot about Rosemary's warnings, the writer's story on the house, the tentacles in her nightmares. She knew she could count on Mehr and felt bad for not contacting her all these years. Anahita did not want history to repeat itself.

What she did not know was that sometimes, history had a way of crawling back into people's lives.

While Anahita was still looking at Mehr's message, the phone rang. An unknown number. Anahita answered. 'Hello?'

'Is this Anahita Anand?'

'Yes, who is this?'

'Hira. Hira Tejwani.'

27

Tea Aur Coffee, Bandra

ANAHITA CALLED HER HUSBAND TO INFORM HIM SHE was going to a café in Bandra to meet a friend. He was busy in some meeting and didn't really care much about her engagements. But he did ask her to share her location with him on WhatsApp, just to be safe. Keshav drove her to the café and waited outside, checking some forwarded videos.

Inside the café, Anahita found Hira Tejwani waiting for her. He was young, in his late twenties, with long dark hair, a grizzly brown beard and tanned skin. He wore a baggy black T-shirt and jeans.

'*Hira Tejwani* never goes to meet his fans, but this is a special case.'

Anahita found it both annoying and amusing that the man referred to himself in third person. 'Thanks a lot. When I saw that you have written something about the house, I wanted to know.'

'Oh! So haven't you read my book yet?' He looked disappointed. 'It is there on Kindle.'

'No, not really. I messaged as soon as I saw the book listing. But I promise, I will order a copy tonight.'

A waiter arrived with a tray of orders. Anahita leaned away from the table, allowing the waiter to place the cup of coffees on the table. Hira picked up the sandwich that he had ordered and wolfed it down as if he had not eaten in days.

'Tell me, why do you want to know about the place?' Bits of lettuce flashed through the gaps in his extraordinarily large teeth.

'I live in 7E, Paradise Heights.'

Hira stopped chewing and stared at her as if nothing else mattered in the world anymore.

'Are you for real?'

'Yes. I have had some weird experiences in that house. I want to know what happened there.' Anahita watched Hira gulp down the sandwich that was in his mouth.

After a moment of anticipation, he said, '7E, Paradise Heights was home to a woman called … ' – he took another bite of the sandwich – ' … Parizaad.'

'Parizaad?' Anahita repeated.

Hira nodded. 'The woman lived alone. Sometimes, her boyfriend – or maybe it was her husband? – would come to visit her. Her family had ousted her because she had joined a dark cult called *Bruja Shamana* and used to sleep around for money … until she got pregnant. She blackmailed the father of the child and got herself that apartment. But then, she started going crazy.'

Anahita was trying to keep up. 'Bruj—what?'

'Bruja Shamana. It was a cult born in India. Few people know about it. In fact, it started long back and some of the most prominent industrialists and people from the entertainment industry are part of this cult. Anyone who joins the cult must renounce all forms of religion and drink a virgin's blood every night, blended with myristicin, a natural hallucinogenic compound. That probably had something to do with Parizaad's eventual insanity. One day, she sacrificed her own daughter to their deity and ate the dead girl's flesh.'

'What?' Anahita was shocked.

'And then she shot herself. It was part of the cult's ritual to attain salvation.'

'Did she leave a note or something behind?'

'Not really.'

'Then how did you know it was a ritual?'

'I know coz I am the expert here. Hira Tejwani is the number one paranormal expert.'

'I am not doubting that, Mr Tejwani.' Anahita tried her best to be polite.

'You shouldn't, lady.'

'But how did you know so much about the woman and the girl? I tried searching all over the internet but there isn't any news article about the incident.'

'It happened in 1999. Internet wasn't a consumer thing in India.'

'Yes, that explains the broken links.'

'Absolutely. All those old news links must be on expired servers. I had visited the place some years ago – part of my investigation. Nobody let me inside, but a lovely lady next door told me whatever she could. The rest I gathered based on my research and expertise in the paranormal field. Did you know I am the founder of Foundation for Indian Paranormal Research?'

You're probably the only member, Anahita thought grimacing on the inside. Out loud she said, 'No' and quickly redirected the conversation back to the house. 'Was the lady Rosemary Woodhouse?'

'That Anglo-Indian lady? Yeah, that was her all right. Does she still live there?'

'She lives in 7D.'

'She did not meet me at the apartment. People are all hush-hush about the place and the incident. If you ask that stupid old watchman, he tells you that nothing ever happened there. Freaking liars!'

The waiter arrived at the table asking if they wanted anything else. Anahita looked at Hira, who shrugged. She asked the waiter to clear the table and bring her the cheque.

After the waiter left, Anahita turned to Hira again and said, 'I saw a woman at the balcony a couple of nights ago. And yesterday, I had a terrible dream. Every night something weird happens...'

'Do you want me to investigate your house for a paranormal presence?'

'Would you do that?'

'Sure. But I charge.' Hira knew when he saw a vulnerable customer. Like a scavenging hyena, he played on Anahita's fears and doubts.

'I will pay whatever you ask, but I want you to come right away, you know, before my husband comes. He wouldn't approve of this.'

'I need to pick up some stuff from my place first. Do you have a car?' the investigator asked.

'Yes, I will take you.'

'Cool! Let us go then.'

Anahita and Hira went to his place first. While Anahita waited in the cab with Keshav, Hira went inside to collect his gear. Varun called in to check if she was all right. He had just gotten out of his meeting.

'I am all right. I am heading home now,' she told her husband over the phone.

'Great! Can you send Keshav after you reach home?' Varun asked.

'I don't know.' Anahita looked at the driver, who was standing outside the car. 'I might need him again.'

Varun paused briefly and spoke to someone. Then he said to Anahita, 'It is okay, darling. I have got another cab here. I have a meeting in Versova at six. Will head home after that. Would you like to go out for dinner?'

Varun's question surprised Anahita, because he hadn't taken her out to dinner in almost a year now. She said, 'Okay.'

'Great, I will call you as soon as my next meeting gets over.'

After disconnecting the call, Anahita checked her Instagram. There were no new messages from Mehr. She locked the phone and kept it back inside her purse. The gate of the residential society opened and out came the paranormal investigator with a huge black bag, the kind used by delivery executives. He placed it on the backseat next to Anahita and himself sat on the front seat next to Keshav. Soon, the driver started the car, and they were off to Paradise Heights.

28

MNP Headquarters

THE PRESENTATION ON HIS MacBook WAS JUST A formality. Varun felt no real need for it. He did not want the reports and newspaper cuttings that he had laid out on the table. Those were there just to create an impression. The effort impressed Bhau, but he awaited eagerly for Varun to reveal his big breaking news.

'Did you see that?' Varun pointed towards a printed report that showed some transaction details. Bhau tried to fathom what the numbers meant. 'These are money transfers from NRI accounts to an NGO called Sanraksha. And guess who runs that NGO?'

Bhau looked at Varun cluelessly.

'Savita Devi.'

'Who is that?'

'Savita Devi is the maternal aunt of the current chief minister's driver. Guess what's even more interesting?' Varun toiled with excitement. 'She died five years ago.'

'I hope you can prove that.'

'Oh, I can, but I won't. Let the right time come, we will do it. For now, I just want all the attention on this big transaction that is going to happen in the city. The big push for development in Mumbai. You must wonder what Sanraksha, or a dead aunt of the CM's driver, has to do with the city's development propaganda?'

Bhau looked on, waiting for Varun's revelation.

'It is a bribe from someone to the CM. Somebody really wanted a huge infrastructure project. Actually, it is the largest infrastructure project in the state. You know … politicians returning favours to old friends who funded their victory.'

Bhau knew perfectly well what Varun was talking about. In fact, everyone had talked about it in the media. Some leading news channels spoke very highly of the advantages of the project – from employment opportunities it would create for lakhs of daily wage workers to the ease of commutation for travellers. Social media influencers flooded their timelines with hashtags like #PublicTransportStopsPollution, #indiasbiggestmetrostation #greatdaysformumbaikars #MeraMetroMahaan #meraCMmahaan etc. The media houses 'aligned' with the ruling party did everything they could to showcase the project as a step towards increasing the use of public transport and promoting a cleaner environment.

'The Metro Shed Project!' Varun revealed finally.

'Brilliant!' the old politician expressed his joy. 'What is your next step?'

'Let me finish my appointments first. I have a plan of action. We will not expose the corruption first. Let's fiddle with the youth's emotions with a new face of revelation, a young Messiah – Abhinav Deshmukh.'

29

7E, Paradise Heights

Fɪʀsᴛ, Hɪʀᴀ ᴘᴜʟʟᴇᴅ ᴏᴜᴛ ᴀɴ EMF sᴇɴsᴏʀ ғʀᴏᴍ ʜɪs ᴋɪᴛ, followed by weird-looking goggles with some sort of audio receiver on its left side. He wore it around his head. Anahita looked on curiously at the mumbo-jumbo setup. Next to come out of the big black bag was a flashlight.

'This is no ordinary flashlight,' he said, as if he could read Anahita's mind. He added, 'It is an ultraviolet ray dispenser. UV rays can fluoresce visible light in total darkness. You might have seen in films how police can see invisible blood stains by throwing UV light on walls, etc. *The Da Vinci Code*? No?'

Anahita seemed clueless but nodded to get on with the proceedings. Hira pressed a button on the EMF sensor. A beep.

'This is a digital sensor. Most of the paranormal investigators in India still use fake analogue ones. Those can malfunction easily. But this is advanced stuff, professional.

Come with me.' He moved towards the kitchen, holding the EMF sensor in front of him as he walked. Anahita followed.

'What does it do?' She asked.

'It detects erratic energy fluctuations. These ghosts or spirits are nothing but energy. They have an electromagnetic field, and this device detects it. The moment it detects an energy, it will go beep!'

After scanning the kitchen, the living room, and the study room, they moved into the master bedroom. Every time they finished scanning a room, Anahita would ask if he had found anything, but he would just tilt his head. As they passed one room after the other, she felt increasingly uneasy.

'Look, if you are scared, you can wait outside until I complete the scan. It is okay, I have got this.'

'No, I would like to see how it works.'

'You know, sometimes these spirits do not come because they fear the occupants of the house. In fact, half the time they try to scare off new occupants or trespassers only because of fear. Just like animals. It is a defence mechanism.'

'Won't you scare the spirit then?'

'Well, what can I say? I have a knack for befriending spirits.'

He smiled – the ego apparent on his face, even behind that bush for a beard. They entered the bedroom and Hira waved the device as he walked from one corner to the other. Nothing beeped. He arrived at the glass door.

'That's where I saw her,' Anahita said. Every strand of hair on her body stood on end as she mentioned her encounter.

Hira inched closer towards the door. Anahita expected a sound from the instrument that he was carrying. She waited anxiously. Just as he was about to open the glass door, the doorbell rang.

'I will get that,' Anahita said, and went out of the room.

'Get what?' Hira was so engrossed in the investigation, he had missed the sound of the doorbell entirely.

After Anahita left for the door, Hira sighed and quickly opened the backside of the EMF sensor and punched in a numeric code. It returned an error. 'Damn, you stupid thing!' He cursed the device. 'Why did you stop working?'

Outside the glass door, the skies had turned grey again. His device was returning an unusual error.

30

When Anahita opened the door, Mehr stood there, waving at her. It was the second time that week her friend had shown up without notice. 'You didn't message …' Anahita began

'Surprise!' Mehr winked. She definitely looked younger in person than in her Instagram profile picture. 'Can I come in?'

Anahita moved away, allowing her friend to enter the house. She noticed Mehr's silky cherry-coloured stole. 'Wow! This looks lovely.'

'Thanks, needed something to match my glass frames. Besides, it was windy. So, what's happening?' Mehr asked, 'I saw a pair of shoes outside. Is Varun home?'

'No,' Anahita replied as she shut the door behind her.

'Then?'

'A woman's ghost is haunting this house.' Anahita didn't mince any words. That's how she was with Mehr.

'What?'

Anahita pulled Mehr towards the bedroom. 'Come, I will introduce you to …'

Just then Hira came out of the bedroom, bumping into Anahita. The EMF device fell on the floor. As Anahita apologized profusely, Mehr let out a snort. 'Who the fuck is this weirdo?' Hira seemed to take offence to Mehr's blunt rudeness and glared at Anahita. Feeling embarrassed and awkward, Anahita immediately introduced the man to her friend, 'This is Hira Tejwani. Paranormal investigator and writer.'

'Para … what?'

Hira appeared baffled. The device that had fallen started beeping suddenly. The alarm took Anahita by surprise, but Mehr started chuckling.

'Did you find the ghost?' Anahita asked.

'I … I … I think I will go. I will come back another time.' Hira stammered as he pocketed his device. He picked up his bag hastily.

Hira's sudden shiftiness confused Anahita. 'But what happened?'

Before Hira could reply, Mehr interjected. 'Yeah, go away, you fraud. Don't you dare come back to this house to fool my friend again. You understand?' Mehr's tone had changed from mocking to serious.

Hira was already putting on his shoes in haste and yelled from the door, 'You should see a doctor, woman!' Then, he ran out of the house as if he really had seen a ghost, slamming the door shut on the way out.

'And you called this idiot to *exorcise* the haunted house?' Mehr asked, eyebrows raised.

'I swear he is genuine – a little boastful, but genuine. He has even written a book. I don't know why he ran away like that. That sensor was beeping suddenly. Did you see? Maybe it detected a ghost in the house. Maybe he saw the ghost.'

Mehr put her arm on Anahita's shoulder. 'Tell me, what makes you think this house is haunted? Who is haunting you?'

'The woman who committed suicide in this house. Her spirit is haunting me.'

31

The Indie, Versova

VARUN HELD AN UNLIT CIGARETTE IN HIS HAND AND waited outside the building. A couple of girls working at *The Indie* had come out to smoke. They stared at him, wondering why he wasn't lighting his and if he was a creep who had only come to the smoking area to ogle at others. Varun did not mind the stares.

A receptionist came and called out to Varun. 'Mr Anand?'

'Yes?' He turned.

'Madam will see you now. Please come with me.'

Varun threw the cigarette and walked inside. The girls who were smoking rolled their eyes, seeing a completely unused cigarette wasted like that. 'He could have given it to us if he didn't want to smoke,' one of them murmured.

Meanwhile, the receptionist showed Varun the way to the editor's cabin. When he entered, he was caught by surprise for a minute – the woman on the editor's seat had a familiar face.

'Hello, Mr Anand!' The editor greeted. She, too, was trying to place the face that she knew she had seen before.

'Mehrab Hussain … Mehr?' Varun asked in disbelief.

'Varun?' Mehr was in half a mind to kick him out. But she knew she couldn't, since he had come for Bhau's work. She had to bury the demons of the past. Varun Anand was not Anu's husband, but her financier's PR guy. *This meeting is strictly professional.*

'What a small world! Didn't realize we'd meet so soon,' Varun said.

'Me neither. Please, take a seat, Mr Anand.'

'Varun.'

'Mr Anand.' She tried to sound indifferent, but inside she felt tremors. 'Let us get on with our meeting. I have another important appointment after this.'

'Sure, Mehr.'

'Mehrab Hussain, please.'

32

7E, Paradise Heights

ANAHITA OPENED THE BOOK SHE HAD FOUND THE OTHER day in the study room. Mehr waited eagerly. Anahita had told her everything about the woman who committed suicide, the ghost who appeared outside the glass door, the missing daughter, the nightmares and the vulture that made cameos at her balcony. At first, Mehr dismissed them as Anahita's imagination, until Anahita told her about all the strange books in the library and the journal with the brown cover.

On the second page of the book, something was written in blue ink. Anahita could not identify the script. She closed the book and handed it over to Mehr.

Mehr looked at it and said, 'It's Gujarati.'

'Really? Do you know anyone who can read it?'

'Dokh-me-nashini,' Mehr read out

'When did you learn Gujarati?'

Mehr smiled.

Impatiently, Anahita asked, 'Okay, what does it mean?'
'I am not sure.'
'Can you read the rest?'
Mehr moved to the second page. 'It is a name, I think.'
'A name?'
'Yeah,' Mehr said, 'Parizaad.'

33

～

The Indie, Versova

THE MEETING WASN'T COMFORTABLE, BUT IT WAS PART of his work. He expected some warmth from the editor since she was a friend of his wife. However, Mehrab Hussain's reception was the opposite. After coming out of the office, he called his wife as promised. He really wanted to eat at an Italian restaurant. Truth was, he did not want to eat what Anahita made. The aftertaste of the previous night's dal-chawal made him feel sick.

He called Anahita. 'Hi, darling. My meeting just got over. By the way, you won't believe whom I met. I will tell you over dinner, would love to see the surprise on your face. Are you ready?'

～

7E, Paradise Heights

While Mehr sat in a corner trying to decipher the content of the book, Anahita answered on the phone, 'I am so sorry. I forgot about our dinner. Can we do it another night?'

'Why? Is everything all right?' Varun asked.

'Well, actually, my friend Mehr is with me.'

'Mehr?'

'Yes. Remember we met her at the party?'

'What? What do you mean Mehr is with you?'

'Why, what's wrong?'

'Anu, Mehr can't be there with you …'

Through the phone, Anahita heard the shuffling of Varun's feet and the creak of a door opening. He asked someone to take the phone. Anahita held her breath, wondering what her husband was up to, until a woman answered. 'Hello, Anahita?' It was a voice Anahita would always recognize instantly.

'Mehr?' Anahita mumbled.

'Yes, what happened? Is everything okay? Your husband asked me to speak to you.' Mehr's voice sounded tense on the phone.

'But … you are … right here.' The phone slid down Anahita's hand and hit the floor. She stared at the person in front of her. She looked like Mehr; sounded like Mehr. *What on earth … ?* But Anahita was now starting to see that something was off … it was Mehr all right, but too young … almost exactly like the Mehr she remembered from nine years ago. As Anahita stared at this younger version of Mehr, sitting in front of her, the maroon-coloured glasses faded and the cherry stole disappeared. The lingering smile on her face faded, little by little, like pixels of an image, and the person started disintegrating into thin air.

Who was it … this apparition-Mehr, stuck in time. Was it a figment of Anahita's troubled imagination or … a ghost?

Her mouth completely dry, Anahita mumbled, 'No … no, no!'

'It is okay, Anu. Close your eyes,' the fading figure spoke. 'Breathe in … Breathe out. Everything is not under our control.'

Anahita closed her eyes tightly. She realized it was not Mehr in front of her. It was an illusion created from her memory – a hallucination. No wonder Hira had run away. He did not see another woman in the house; what he had actually seen was Anahita acting eerie – switching from timid and polite to cynical and rude.

Anahita pushed her fingers inside her ears, sealing them from every sound that emanated outside – the sound of raindrops, frantic 'hellos', 'are you okay' from the phone on the floor. In the total silence, Anahita could hear her teacher explaining how air entered the alveolar sac. The image of the alveolar sac appeared in the darkness.

Sounds from the past came hurling at her – Keshav shouting at the little boy on the day she arrived in Mumbai, her husband yelling at her for being careless, her mother scolding her for seeing her friend, Hira babbling at the door that she should see a doctor, Dr Malhotra telling her that someday Varun will come to know about the baby … and finally, a scream … the one from the classroom of Good Shepherd's Convent in 2005.

It was Mehr's scream, as she struggled against Christopher's attempt to rape her.

13 August 2005, Saturday
Good Shepherd Convent, Gurgaon

When she flung open the door, Anahita saw Mehr lying on the desk, helpless. Christopher, who had Mehr pinned to the ground, looked at Anahita in horror. He had not accounted for this intrusion. Anahita's pulse rate rose, for what she saw made her want to throw up. White hot light flashed before her eyes, blinding her momentarily.

When the flash of light faded, she saw something else. Anahita was no longer in the classroom. Someone was on top of her, pinning her down. She felt a stinging sensation surge in her belly and make its way to her eyes – a searing pain.

A flash of white light.

She was in the classroom again, with Mehr holding out her hand, crying for help. Christopher charged towards Anahita. Instinctively, Anahita went for her bag lying on the desk and pulled out her geometry box. She took out the compass and as Christopher reached to grab her, she drove it into his left eye – the one with the scar above it. The boy yelled in agony. Anahita pulled the compass out, sending drops of red plunging through white viscous fluid in his eye.

Another flash of white swept across her vision.

When it faded, she was back in the other room, where the shadowy figure was still on top of her, trying to strangle her. Anahita screamed. The compass still in her hand, she plunged it into her attacker's chest. The figure let go of her ... and there was the flash of white light again.

When the flash faded, she was in the classroom again. Mehr trying to get up on her feet, but her injury would not let her. Near Anahita's feet lay an unconscious Christopher, the compass upright in his chest. Maroon blood spilled from his chest and pooled under him. And then Anahita saw the same colour streaming down her thighs – she had attained puberty on that ill-fated day.

Anahita fainted. The smudged diagram of the alveoli sac was the last thing she saw.

Part II

The Tower of Silence

34

❧

13 August 2019, Tuesday
Fortune Hospital, Bandra

I*T IS YOU AND ONLY YOU. I DO NOT EXIST, ANAHITA. I DO NOT exist.* That was what Anahita had heard imaginary Mehr say when they were standing at their balcony a couple of days ago. Or was that a week ago? Anahita did not remember. When she opened her eyes, she was at a hospital and it felt like some days had passed. When the blurring of her eyes finally wore out, she saw the beautiful-looking woman standing in front of her. It was Mehr, quite different from how she appeared last time; she looked older with no glasses, just like she looked at Bhau's party.

'Are you … real?' Anahita asked in a frail voice as she tried to lift her head.

'Relax, Anahita. Don't stress yourself,' Mehr said as she came near Anahita's bed, 'I am really here. You are not hallucinating, Anu.'

Anahita touched her forehead and felt a bandage wound over her head tightly.

'You fell and hit your head on the shelf, and it fell down on you,' Mehr revealed to her friend. 'When we got there, you had lost a lot of blood as well.'

'Wow! I thought that we had caught up on a lot of things happening in my life. How could I not see it? You looked so young, just like back in the day.' She tried to recollect.

'The mind plays tricks on you when you let it take over.'

'Where is Varun?' Anahita asked.

'I … I think he must be around.'

Anahita sighed. 'He went back to work, didn't he?'

'No, I am sure he is here. I came just ten minutes ago. He left only after that. Probably to see the doctor. Or maybe he went for a smoke?'

'He doesn't smoke … not anymore. Just pretends … like he pretends we are married.'

Anahita looked around. The hospital room was white except for the maroon accents here and there. The rays of the sun coming through the parted curtain made her feel like the monsoons were finally over. Had she been unconscious for that long a time? She looked down at her stomach … *What happened to my baby?* She sat up with a jerk, her heart racing. When she touched her belly, it felt flat.

'Where is my baby? What happened to my baby?' Anahita cried out in distress. Giving no consideration to the IV needle in her arm, she tried to stand up. The sudden movement ripped the needle from her arm, and the drip stand crashed, the bottle shattering into tiny pieces. Mehr tried to stop her, but Anahita had already raced to the door, dragging the mess behind her.

Varun was entering the room at that very moment. The door swung open in his face and out came a panicked Anahita. When she saw her husband, she grabbed him and started to yell. 'Where's my baby, Varun? What happened to my baby?'

'What baby?'

'Our baby … ' Anahita said, her heart sinking, tears flooding down her cheeks, blood from her vein.

It was the first time Varun had heard about the baby, and the news shook him to the core.

35

14 August 2019, Wednesday
Dr Shetty's Clinic

WHILE ANAHITA WAS UNCONSCIOUS AT THE HOSPITAL, Varun called up Dr Malhotra and informed her about the recent developments. She recommended they consult a neuropsychiatrist after Anahita was discharged from the hospital, and referred them to one of her old colleagues, Dr Nidhi Shetty. She had mentioned that Shetty was their best bet at such a stage, now that Anahita was hallucinating.

Dr Shetty's clinic was on the floor above her residence in Juhu, where she would consult between 6 and 10 p.m. She did not see over ten patients in a day at the clinic. It was difficult to get an appointment, but Dr Malhotra's phone call got them one. Certificates of excellence that the doctor had received over the years covered the walls of her consultation room. Enormous volumes of medical journals embraced the shelves behind her. She went through the report Dr Malhotra had emailed her about Anahita. In between, she checked the medical report and fMRI scans sent by the hospital.

After she had gone through all the data, she turned towards the nervous couple sitting on the other side of her desk. 'I would like to speak with Mrs Anand, in private.' She looked at Varun. 'I hope you won't mind waiting outside.'

'Sure,' Varun said and left the room.

—⁂—

Varun waited in the empty hall for the next twenty minutes. The assistant had left after the last patient of the day. Only Varun, Anahita and Dr Shetty remained in the clinic. Varun's phone constantly buzzed with messages from his office. He had a huge week ahead. His team was in touch with all the big activists of the state, social media influencers, and digital marketing agencies. His toolkit was ready to mobilize a mammoth crowd to kickstart Abhinav Deshmukh's political campaign. He had a lot on his mind, and his wife's condition was the last thing he wanted to handle right now.

Twenty minutes later, Anahita came out of the room. She informed Varun that Dr Shetty wanted to talk to him alone. It was Anahita's turn to wait outside.

—⁂—

'I will ask some private questions. Please don't feel uncomfortable,' Dr Shetty told Varun, glancing at the notes she had taken while interviewing Anahita. She sounded stern.

'I … I will try my best,' Varun replied.

'Good. Anahita mentioned that you knew her for three years before you got married to her.'

'Well, I had known her through a common family friend. I had a crush on her back then.'

'Back then?'

'It started as a crush when I moved to Gurugram.'

'When was this?'

'2015. She lived next door. My mother became friends with Anahita's. Although our families were involved, I did the talking – the proposal and all. I liked her. She never objected either. We dated for some time before getting married. I thought it was important that both of us spent time with each other before … you know … getting hitched …'

'But?'

' … but she was different.'

'She did not want to have sex before marriage?'

'She said she was not comfortable. I … I respected that. She hid nothing from me. She told me about *the incident* that happened in high school, and I was so madly in love with her, it didn't bother me. I thought she would feel secure after marriage.' Varun sighed. 'But then … we got married and nothing changed. She would not let me near her … you know … *sexually*. It wasn't until 2017, when she got drunk at a party. After that we had sex for the first time. Alcohol helped her suppress the trauma or whatever stopped her from having sex. She started drinking every time we wanted to have sex.'

'We or *you* … wanted to have sex?'

Varun averted his eyes, nodding slightly. He nodded his head in agreement.

'All right. Then, can you tell me why you don't want to have a baby?'

'It's not that I *don't*. I was just not ready – career-wise. Besides, I wanted her to be better before we had a child. I had faith in Dr Malhotra's treatment … but I guess it wasn't working.'

'Mr Anand, do you know why she started drinking?'

'I think I already told you.'

'Well, no. She started drinking because that was the only way she could have a baby. She wanted to have a real biological connection. But she was afraid to have sex – genophobia, as you must already know. One of the many phobias that your wife has. When sober, she could not even withstand the sight of a naked man, let alone have sex with him. The trauma from the attempted rape she witnessed in school was that severe. On top of that, she was on anti-depressants regularly, which has taken its toll on her mind. She suffers from complex PTSD and anxiety disorders. She has been pregnant for almost ten weeks now. Did you have any idea, Mr Anand?'

'I … I … no.'

'To compensate for the lack of sex-life, you kept yourself busy with your career. You were punishing your wife by isolating her completely. Despite knowing what she went through. I will not accuse any further because that is not my job. But I am going to tell you my diagnosis.'

Varun waited for the woman to begin. He felt guilty, but he still believed that his reason for not having a baby was justifiable. The doctor removed her glasses, placed them folded on the notes and then looked at Varun.

'In the past, Dr Malhotra had treated Anahita for Schizophrenia. She was able to control it to a great extent, and she was doing a great job tackling the depression and anxiety disorders too.' A pause. 'Schizophrenia,' she began, 'can be the after effect of an emotional trauma, a brain injury, or it can even be hereditary. I doubt it is genetic in Anahita's case, but she had an accident when she was a child. She was hit by a car and she had a traumatic brain injury from the accident. The TBI did permanent damage to her right amygdala.'

'Amygdala?'

'Yes, it is that part of the brain that controls emotions related to fear and sadness. This part is directly associated with *conditioned fear* and represents a core fear system in the human body, which is involved in the expression of that *conditioned fear*. We measure fear by noting changes in autonomic activity including increased heart rate, increased blood pressure, as well as in simple reflexes such as flinching or blinking. It can take the form of different phobias. I have found some patterns of conditioned fear based on my interview with your wife and Dr Malhotra's patient records.

'Did you know your wife attained puberty late in her life? According to what I have read from her history sent by Dr Malhotra, the problems started after the emotional trauma inflicted by the stabbing incident in 2005, which coincided with her first period. She stabbed a boy because she saw him raping her best friend. She had acted in self-defence, but the trauma stayed. She had seen so much blood that day that shades of red and maroon trigger the conditioned stimulus. Also, every time you made a sexual advance towards her, Anahita's mind floods with images of bursting alveoli sacs.'

'Alveoli sacs? Why …'

'Apparently, it was drawn on the blackboard in her class. After she stabbed the boy, the diagram was the last thing she saw before she fainted. Sex is the trigger, the conditioned fear. The routine combination of alcohol and the anti-depression drug gave her relief from this. Her desire to have a baby and guilt for not fulfilling your desire made her eager to ignore the health repercussions. But it has taken a toll on her brain.

'You had already given up on her. When she found out that she was pregnant, she was afraid to tell you. She thought you did not love her anymore and that you would not let her keep the baby. In fact, that is what she thought when she got up at the hospital yesterday. She thought you aborted her baby while she was unconscious. When you came to Mumbai, good old memories started coming back and coincidentally, she met the person who wove all those memories – Mehr. Anahita just wanted someone to talk to, she just wanted someone to hear her feelings and insecurities. She did not have Dr Malhotra here, and you had isolated her so much that her mind, out of desperation, created a long-lost friend from figments of her memory. She started seeing and hearing Mehr. This imaginary friend would come every time Anahita wanted to talk about something that bothered her. Consider it fortunate that we found out in the initial stages. Your wife now knows that she was seeing an imaginary person. She has even seen an imaginary vulture. This is good, because she is aware of her condition; many patients don't even realize it and live in complete denial and end up harming themselves or others.'

'What do we do now, Dr Shetty?'

'Your wife isn't well. She needs help. I would suggest that you take her back to Gurugram. She needs to be under the treatment of Dr Malhotra.'

'Can't you see her?'

'I do not have the bandwidth, I'm afraid.'

'Any medication?'

'Since she is pregnant, I can't even prescribe any medications. She needs your time. The more you ignore her, the worse the situation will become. Schizophrenia sounds scary, but many people with this condition manage to lead almost normal lives. She managed in the past, but something has triggered it again after coming to Mumbai. Medicines can only give symptomatic relief, what she actually needs is your support.'

'I … I am in the middle of a big assignment right now. I can't go back to Gurugram. I won't be able to …'

'Look, things could get complicated in the final trimester. Do this. Get this friend of her, Mehr, to come and see her. You can try calling your in-laws to Mumbai. As for medications, I will not give her any anti-psychotic. There are some yoga and meditation techniques that she can try at home under the guidance of a professional. It should keep her calm in the short run. However, if she has another such episode, then you have to get her back to Dr Malhotra. All right?'

'Yes, doctor.'

'Don't feel guilty now. I know our careers are important, but sometimes you must look beyond that. You said that you had loved her, once. Look deep inside yourself … that love must still be there somewhere … get that out and do the right thing.' The doctor handed over the prescription to Varun and smiled.

'Of course, doctor. Thank you.'

~

When Varun came out, Anahita was waiting expectantly. He put his arm around her and gently squeezed her arm. As the two left the clinic, Varun found himself wishing that he had not come to Mumbai. He had forgotten about the toolkit for Abhinav's campaign. He wished he could go back to Gurugram with Anahita. But he knew he could not do that because he was stuck in Bhau's invisible line of control.

36

7E, Paradise Heights
9 p.m.

AFTER PUTTING ANAHITA TO SLEEP, VARUN STAYED UP. He went through the toolkit, and all the content that his social media team had approved. They had scheduled over a thousand tweets with the hashtag #MumbaiEnvironmentCrisis for posting at midnight, followed by a drip-campaign with twenty posts after every two minutes interval until noon. The first one, however, would come from Abhinav's personal Twitter account. So, when the Twitterverse tracked the source of the information, they would see the fresh face of environmental activism – Abhinav Deshmukh. To back up, there would be timely interviews and reports on the news channels, papers, and digital media agencies that Varun had already tapped in. That was his master-plan, an aggressive version of what he did during the Delhi elections. He knew it would work, but his wife's condition made him a little jittery. He went to the balcony. With an unlit cigarette in his hand, he looked at the contact list on his phone. At such times he knew there was only one person he could call.

'Hi, Mr Desai.'

'Hi, beta. How are you? All set?'

'Yes, everything is going as per plan.'

'What happened, Varun? You sound low. What's wrong?'

'It is my wife, Anahita.'

'What happened to her?'

'She has started hallucinating again. I … I am partly at fault.'

'Come now, don't blame yourself, son.' There was that father-like warmth in Desai's voice. He coughed once.

'I haven't given her any attention in a long time. The doctor says that it has taken a toll on her mind. I think I'll need some time off … after this campaign,' Varun said, his voice dripping with guilt.

'Why wait till then?'

'I just started this campaign. They need me here.'

'So does your wife. If I were you, I would not be thinking about my career, you know. Besides, I know how capable you are. I won't stop funding Tinsel just because you decide to spend some time with your wife. You can hire an interim operating officer who will work for you.'

'I don't think Bhau would let me do that. I am *sure* he won't.'

'If you can't, I can try talking to him.'

'No, it is okay. I will talk to him tomorrow.'

'Good! Just let me know how it goes, okay?'

'Yes, I will.'

'And don't feel embarrassed to ask if you need anything. Just ask!'

Desai's benevolent voice calmed Varun.

'Thank you. Thank you for the concern. Goodnight, Mr Desai.' Varun wished he could call the old man *papa*.

'Goodnight *beta*!'

37

A NAHITA SLEPT WELL BECAUSE SHE WAS TIRED. SHE HAD
not slept like that ever since they had moved to Mumbai.
It seemed long, but it had only been about two weeks.

When Varun's alarm went off, she got up too, but strangely
she could not move. She was on her back, eyes open and
staring at the ceiling. She could not feel her body at all – sleep
paralysis. She wanted to scream and alert her husband, who
had gone to the bathroom to brush his teeth. But she could
not move her mouth, nor her tongue. At the periphery of her
vision, the curtains to the balcony parted and the glass door
opened. Anahita felt a shadow hovering above her feet; it
drew closer to reveal the apparition – this time, a rotting body
inside her tattered maroon dress. Maggots wove in and out of
the pores of her decomposing skin. Anahita knew her. It was
the woman she saw outside the glass door – it was Parizaad.
The rotting ghost crawled above a helpless Anahita stuck on
the bed, until its face was right above Anahita's. It gawked
at Anahita's immobile eyes, and then suddenly, it sank into
Anahita's body. Anahita felt a thumping sensation somewhere
inside her soul as darkness took over her surroundings.

When the darkness faded, Anahita realized she was standing up. She could feel her arms, legs and every inch of her body. Everything around her appeared reddish, as if in an altered state of existence. Was it another dream? Was she in a coma? A large gate stood majestically in front of her. It had a huge lock on it. She looked around; tall trees stared at her diabolically. Through the gaps in the canopy of trees, she could see the cloudy sky.

A deafening silence surrounded her as she walked on a path that led her to an enormous tower. It was old, and she heard a vulture approaching from behind, hitting her with its talons before crashing into the rocky ground. The vulture struggled to breathe. As Anahita kneeled to take a closer look at the vulture, a rotting hand crawled out of the ground and caught her by the right ankle. The nails grew and plunged into her skin. She cried in pain.

'Don't leave me … Anahita …' a ghastly voice hissed into Anahita's ears. 'Help me …'

15 August 2019, Thursday
11:30 a.m.

When Anahita woke up, it was late in the morning. Her memory of last night was fuzzy. She found inexplicable bruise marks on her right ankle. The chants of *help me* and *don't leave me Anahita* reverberated inside her head. Her vision was blurry from deep slumber. Near the window, she saw a woman's hazy figure. Anahita recoiled in fright. The figure got up and walked towards Anahita.

'Relax. It is me, Mehr. The real one,' the woman said as she came into sight.

Anahita noted the short haircut; *it was the real Mehr*.

'Come now, wash your face. Freshen up.'

'How did you …'

'How did I come here?'

Anahita nodded.

'Well, Varun called me in the morning. I hope you know by now that we are colleagues as well.'

'I guess …' Anahita tried to remember.

'Small world, what else can I say?' Mehr smiled gently. Anahita responded with a forceful one. 'Varun asked if I could stay with you. He thought you would be more comfortable with me than that driver … Keshav.'

'Work comes first for him, as always!'

'It is really important, trust me; I know what he is doing. He can't afford to miss it now.' Mehr touched Anahita's right cheek with her hand. 'How are you feeling today, Anu?'

'I had a dream. A bad one. Again.'

'Do you want to talk about it?'

It suddenly dawned on Anahita that everything she had disclosed so far was to the imaginary Mehr. 'I guess we'll have to start over.'

38

MNP Headquarters

'OUR HASHTAG IS TRENDING WITH OVER TWENTY-three thousand tweets within ten hours since the first tweet from Abhinav,' Varun said, looking at the senior politician's nephew seated next to him. 'I am expecting two more write-ups on the issue from *The Indie* and *Swaraj Post* before ten. That will take us high on the ladder, and by evening, our cause will be the point of discussion on prime-time debates. We already have an arrangement with *Nation Today*, but others will also catch up if it trends well.' Varun turned towards Bhau, who was sitting on his throne-like cushioned seat. 'If the ruling party's spokesperson does not respond on Twitter, then I will require Abhinav to tweet that he will sit on a dharna at the site. He'll go live on Instagram later in the night where he can call our supporters. My team will do the rest tomorrow.'

'Brilliant!' Bhau said.

Immersed in his phone, Abhinav said, 'I think it is awesome. I have never got so many retweets and comments on my post … ever! You are a magician, man!'

Varun smiled, but Bhau had noticed he was not really in his element that morning. When Abhinav stepped out of the room for a call, Bhau turned to Varun. 'What happened, Varun? You look so dull.'

Varun told him about his wife, glossing over the fact that he wanted to take some time off from the campaign. The campaign had only begun, and it was unethical of him to leave at that stage. But his wife's re-ignited condition was also at the same initial stage.

After quietly listening to Varun's dilemma, Bhau finally said, 'I can understand what you're going through. In fact, I went through similar phases in the initial stages of my political career. These challenges will weigh you down, you know, you can sink and hit the bottom … if we had not risen against our oppressors then we wouldn't be celebrating our seventy-second Independence Day today,' he said, trying to appeal to the ambitious side of Varun. 'You are at a critical stage in your career; if you sink here, then you may never get up again.' The words sounded more like a threat coming from Bhau. 'I don't think you have to go back to Delhi. We have excellent doctors here. What was her name, you said?'

'Dr Shetty.' Varun answered.

'Yes, Shetty. If you like her, then I will make it so that she cancels all her appointments and only tends to your wife. Don't you worry. I can do that. As for the house. I am aware of the suicide that happened there, and if you think it is affecting your wife, why don't you shift here? The top floor is unutilized. I can ask Keshav to prepare it for you to move in.

Nobody goes there. I will make sure that your wife gets food whenever she needs. You can also concentrate on work and tend to your wife whenever you want.'

'No, that won't be necessary. We will manage there.'

'As you see fit. As for a caretaker, I think Keshav will be perfect for that role. Let him stay there during the day. He can be in the car at your designated parking spot – just a call away. If need be, we can have CCTV cameras to monitor your wife at all times.'

'All right, sure. That sounds good. Probably won't need the CCTV though.'

'This is the least I can do for you. I just want you to concentrate on this campaign while I take care of your *insignificant* problems. All right? These favours are never wasted; trust me when I say this.'

'Yes, I do.'

'Good. I have some urgent work now. If you'll excuse me.'

'Yes, of course. I will see you in the evening. Please don't forget about your prime-time appearance tonight. My content guy will send you a draft of things that you have to speak on the tele.'

'Thank you, Varun,' Bhau said with a warm smile, 'Happy Independence Day!'

After Varun left, Bhau made a couple of phone calls. One was to Dr Shetty's hospital and the other one to Keshav. Bhau instructed Keshav to keep a watch over Anahita as the big man had promised Varun. Few minutes later, Varun also received a message from Dr Shetty, saying that she would see Anahita. Bhau had resolved Varun's concerns. It was time for him to keep his promise and propel Abhinav to stardom.

39

———

7E, Paradise Heights

AT FIRST, MEHR DID NOT UNDERSTAND WHAT ANAHITA meant when she said that she had to start over. Then, bit by bit, Anahita told her about all the things that had happened to her in the last few years first, eventually coming to the strange events of the past few weeks, since they had moved into Paradise Heights. Anahita showed Mehr the spot where she saw the woman's ghost and gave Mehr the book with the brown cover. The two women sat on the floor and explored the contents of the book.

'What's written on the cover?' Mehr opened the book inquisitively.

'I don't know, but … well, the imaginary Mehr could read Gujarati.' Anahita chuckled. 'Can you believe it? She said the title of the journal was *Dokhmenashini*.'

'She was part of your imagination. So everything she knew or said must have come from your subconscious mind.'

'My subconscious? What does that mean?'

'That means you must have learnt Gujarati at some point.'

'Nope! Not a chance! The only Gujarati I know is from a daily soap that mom used to watch, and probably a little from *Kal Ho Na Ho*.'

'Oh God! Anu, I just remembered we went for that movie at DT City Center.'

'Yeah! You said SRK was *the best*, and we danced in the theatre to "*It's the time to disco*".'

Mehr looked into Anahita's eyes. 'Oh Anu! How inseparable were we back then!'

'Well, according to Dr Shetty, I created a whole imaginary version of you.' Anahita smiled, but her eyes were moist.

'I am glad we caught the imaginary Mehr before she could take over your life.' Mehr wiped Anahita's eyes. 'And no, I can't read Gujarati. But I can send a screenshot to a friend who can help.'

'Wow! That is exactly what I had suggested to imaginary Mehr that day.'

Mehr laughed again. She clicked a picture of the scribbling and sent it to her friend over WhatsApp. The response came within minutes.

'What is it, tell me?'

Mehr showed her the phone. The message read:

It is a name. Parizaad.

The two gazed at each other in disbelief.

'So … what the imaginary Mehr read was true?'

'It seems to be that way.' Mehr quickly flipped through the pages. A sudden realization hit her. Mehr glanced at Anahita and said, 'Fish! This just confirms my theory. There is knowledge of Gujarati in your memories, probably repressed ones.'

'Not possible! Maybe that Mehr really was a ghost, and the ghost knew Gujarati.'

'Come on, Anahita. You don't actually believe that. And if it *was* a ghost – if ghosts are real – then why would it assume my form?' Mehr flipped through the book and noticed an inland letter stuck between two pages. 'Look!' she exclaimed peeling out the blue inland letter. 'It is a letter, an unsent one. It's empty, but there is an address.' She flipped it over and read from the cover, 'Mr Ferozie Irani, 13/B, Sheila Cooperative Society, Bombay-02.'

'Why is the letter blank?'

'Maybe she died before she could write it.'

'Do you think we can find this person at the address?'

'I don't know. It has been twenty years. He could be dead for all we know.'

'I want to find out.'

'No, Anahita! You don't have to do that.'

'Mehr, please. I honestly believe that there is a wandering spirit in this house and my heart tells me it wants me to go there.' Anahita remembered how desperate the ghastly voice had sounded in the dream she had in the morning. 'It is okay if you don't want to get involved.'

Mehr sighed. 'I guess I can go with you. Besides, I have time till five in the evening. I will book a cab for us.'

'No, I can ask Keshav to take us.'

'All right, let us do this.'

Mehr was sceptical but thought that if they went to the place and learnt nothing, it might put an end to Anahita's delusional curiosity. Anahita was just happy that her friend agreed to help her. And so they set out.

40

Sheila Cooperative Society

'*AREY SUN*,' KESHAV CALLED OUT TO A LITTLE BOY wearing a tattered vest, '*Yeh address bata kidhar hain. Sheila Cooperative Society.*'

The little boy pointed towards a cluster of old buildings that appeared like matchboxes decked against each other.

'*Chal phut ab*,' the driver said and steered the car in the direction of the building. He looked twice at the rear-view mirror. The two women sitting in the back had been chatting ever since they entered the car.

The car stopped in front of the building. 'Madam, I will be nearby. Please call me when you are done and I will come to pick you up from here,' Keshav said.

When Anahita looked outside, she saw the board that read *Sheila Cooperative Society*. She felt like she had been there before. The visuals looked very familiar.

Noticing the change on Anahita's face, Mehr asked, 'What is it?'

'I … I feel like I have come here before.'

'Madam … ' the driver cut in. 'You came here earlier in the week, remember? I had dropped you on the other end of this road … when you came to buy curtains for the bedroom.'

'Oh, yes. I … I remember now.'

'But why did you come this far? The shops were on that side.'

'I … I must have wandered off. I think I was looking for a restaurant,' she said dismissively. She did not remember things clearly. Anahita stepped out of the car and stood looking at the big board.

Why does this board look so familiar? Did I come here that day? She wondered if she had fainted on that very spot. She started fidgeting, beads of sweat appeared on her forehead. *Did I feel like I had seen this before that day too?* Questions popped in her head like kernels of corn in a hot oven.

As Keshav started the car and drove away, Mehr and Anahita walked inside the B block. Looking for a place to park, Keshav wondered what Anahita was up to. He was growing suspicious of her activities. Bhau had asked him to keep an eye on her because she was not well, but he wondered if that was the whole story. In carrying out Bhau's order, perhaps he could satisfy his own curiosity as well. Once parked, Keshav walked towards the building to follow Anahita.

41

FEROZIE WAS A TALL MAN IN HIS EARLY SIXTIES. HIS round face sported a thinning grey beard. The old man lived alone in a house that did not boast of luxury. When Mehr and Anahita came knocking at his door, he was getting ready to go out. He welcomed them, and they sat in the small living room. He knew neither of his guests, but he quickly recollected seeing Anahita a few days ago.

'Weren't you the girl who fainted in front of my house that day? It was you, wasn't it?' He asked in his baritone voice.

'I … Yes, I was here.'

'That's why your face looked so familiar. My dear girl, what had happened to you that day?'

'I … I …' Anahita stammered as she struggled to recollect.

The investigative journalist in Mehr engaged with the bait that the old Parsi man had thrown at them. 'What did *you* see that day?'

'Well, I think it was before noon. Quite rainy … not as sunny as today. I was returning home from the inn where I work when I saw this young lady. She passed by me as I arrived at the gate. Then I heard a sound. When I turned around, I saw her lying unconscious on the ground.'

The women's eyes widened with curiosity. Anahita's heart pounded. *Tell me what happened to me. I want to know how I ended up in my home. Who took me home? Was it the ghost?*

'I wanted to help, but before I could' – with a look of amusement on his face, he turned towards Anahita – 'you got up as if nothing had happened. But there was something different about you. You asked me, "Are you all right?" That's what I thought at first, but then you said " … Anahita" and I realized you were not talking to me … perhaps to an invisible person standing between you and me. You even consoled this person, this *Anahita*. "Don't worry … I am here now. Breathe in, breathe out." That's what you said.' The old man paused.

The two women looked at each other in surprise. Anahita and Mehr understood exactly what had happened that day. When Anahita fainted, imaginary Mehr took over as the alternate personality and dragged the worn-out Anahita back home. But in reality, both persons were one, and all of that was being done by Anahita. That was what Ferozie had seen.

'Who's Anahita?' Ferozie asked.

'I am,' Anahita said.

'Why were you calling out to yourself? Are you well, my dear?'

'It is a little complicated,' Mehr replied.

'I see. And why are you here today? Did you lose something that day?' Ferozie asked, glancing at his wristwatch. 'I have to go somewhere, you know.'

'Well, we actually wanted to ask you about something else.' Mehr took over. She pulled out the inland letter that she had found in the book and handed it over to the old man.

The old man took the blue piece of folded paper. 'That is my address. I haven't seen these in years. Who uses inland letters these days, anyway? Where did you find this?'

'It was in my house.' Anahita informed, 'We think it belongs to the woman who lived there before me. She lived there a long time ago, maybe twenty years or so …'

'What woman?' Ferozie asked. There was an edge in his voice as he studied the peculiar handwriting on the front.

'A woman called Parizaad.'

The name ran his blood cold. The veins in his eyes popped red. He threw the inland on the floor, and growled, 'Get the hell out of my house. Don't you dare come back here again. Get out!'

The women jumped up, shocked by the old man's reaction.

'But we just …' Anahita tried to request.

'No!' Ferozie started pushing them out. 'Get out of here before I call the police!'

Anahita and Mehr noticed that the man was almost on the verge of tearing up. 'Sorry, sorry sir, we are leaving.' Mehr picked up the crumpled letter from the floor and left with Anahita. The old man shut the door as soon as they stepped outside. Ferozie's reaction took the women by surprise.

'What happened, madam? Everything okay? Why was the old man shouting?' Keshav, who was waiting outside, asked with serious concern.

'Yes, we are fine. Let's go,' Anahita said.

The women started walking. Keshav was right behind them, ready to guard them if anyone came attacking; after all, Bhau had given him a responsibility. As they reached the car, Mehr whispered in Anahita's ear, 'He seems to know something. We will follow him.'

42

After lying low for ten minutes, Anahita and Mehr observed Ferozie leaving in an old Chetak scooter. A cloth bag filled with a cuboidal package rested on the floor mat between his legs. Keshav chased him as Ferozie crossed the Chhatrapati Shivaji Terminus Railway Station. The traffic was sparse and lot of police deployment all over because it was 15 August.

Ferozie took a right from Dadabhai Naoroji Road onto Walchand Hirachand Marg before making a U-turn at St Georges Road. Keshav followed the path closely but lost him to an incoming truck that overtook them suddenly at the signal. The car came to a screeching halt at the signal.

'Shit! We have lost him,' Anahita said.

'I think I know where he has gone.' Mehr googled something on her phone. 'Keshav, take a left to Perin Nariman Street.'

'Okay, madam!' the driver said, looking at the rear-view mirror.

As soon as the signal turned green, the car reached the street that connected Walchand Hirachand Marg with Horniman

Circle. Mehr instructed Keshav to pull up somewhere closer to the narrow Agiyari lane. The women got down from the car and walked towards the Agiyari – the Parsi fire temple. Ferozie's scooter was parked on the way, the owner and the bag gone. Anahita and Mehr arrived in front of the temple. The board outside said that it only admitted members of the Parsi community.

'How come you got so interested in this?' Anahita asked Mehr as they waited outside, on the opposite side of the road.

'Honestly, I believed nothing when you said the house was haunted and all. I accompanied you just to prove you wrong. But then that man revealed how you fainted outside his house. It was creepy. I feel there is something more to this entire experience you are having since you came down to Mumbai. When the old guy freaked out at the inland letter, I knew there was a buried mystery in all this. Maybe you are not crazy after all. There is a connection.'

'Maybe the ghost is real,' Anahita said with a smile.

'Well … if the ghost is a secret from the past, then yes, the ghost as a metaphor could be real. Otherwise, I really don't believe in paranormal or supernatural entities.' Mehr chuckled as she recollected one incident that Anahita had narrated at brunch earlier in the day, 'You should probably consult that guy with the ghost-detecting machine again.'

'Hira Tejwani?'

'Yes, that one. I had done a story on my website a couple of months ago exposing people who falsely claimed to be psychic mediums, ghost hunters, exorcists, etc. Hira was also part of that list.'

'I had many questions that needed answers,' Anahita said.

'Do you know what I called them in that story of mine?'

'What?'

Mehr grinned. '*Suit-boot vale tantric.* I will send a link to you. Try reading that.'

'You're so mean. I think everyone has a right to pursue what they believe.'

'As long as they are not forcing their beliefs on vulnerable people. Ordinary people just want to live a simple life, with or without divine forces. When something bad happens, they become vulnerable, and people like Hira try to exploit them. I am not saying that everyone out there is a fraud. For the interview, I spoke to noetic scientists who are researching the existence of ghosts and spirits. But they weren't interested in exploiting the miseries of others. However, because of some mischievous rascals like that Hira, the entire community gets the taint.'

'In short, you are calling me vulnerable.'

'Yes, you are emotionally vulnerable. You have always been,' Mehr said.

The two looked at each other in silence for a few seconds, before Mehr spotted the old man coming out of the gate of a building near the fire temple. It was an old inn.

'There,' Mehr pointed.

Anahita turned. Ferozie also saw the two women standing right across the street staring at him. The bag in his hand was empty.

'You girls again?' He spoke with fury.

Mehr quickly crossed the street and stood in his path. 'Look,' she said softly, hoping that it would calm the hostile old man, 'We just wanted some information that might help my friend here. She is unwell. Please listen to me. If you don't want to talk here, then we can go somewhere in private.'

'No means no. Get out of here!' He shouted and his voice alerted people in the surroundings. The inn's entrance door opened and a tall man in a white shirt stepped out. He was older than Ferozie.

Mehr had already started retreating, walking back to Anahita. 'Don't shout. We are going.'

The tall man behind him asked Ferozie, 'What happened? Who are these girls?'

Ferozie turned around and informed, 'They came to my house and now they have come here. They are asking about her ...'

The tall man's face turned pale as he looked at Anahita and Mehr briskly walking towards their car. They were getting inside and within seconds, the car left the street. The tall man's gaze returned to a nervous Ferozie. He placed his hands on Ferozie's shoulder. 'Don't worry, Ferozie. Go home. I will take care of this.'

43

MEHR INVITED ANAHITA TO COME TO THE STUDIO, where she was going to share the panel with Abhinav and some environmental activists. Varun was at the studio monitoring everything behind the scenes. However, Anahita went home. She wanted to rest. Keshav dropped Mehr at the studio and then drove Anahita to her apartment. He parked the car at the apartment's designated parking space and waited inside.

Varun called once to check if Anahita was all right. He spoke for three minutes on the phone and that was a record. She fathomed her husband was guilt-ridden after seeing Dr Shetty. His morning note that day had a *take care* written on it, followed by a heart shape in the end. He told her on the phone that he was in the news studio with Mehr and others. He said that it was a big night as it was the end of the first leg of his campaign. She said she would tune into the news channel at nine.

There was still time for the prime-time debate, so she started going through the contents of the big brown book in the library. It was mostly written in Gujarati script,

179

except for the few English words that appeared once in a while. She stopped at the diagram of the circular structure. Anahita clicked a photo of the diagram on her phone and then uploaded it on Google. The image search returned her with some interesting matches. She clicked on one of them, and it led to an online encyclopaedia. The page's title: *Tower of Silence.*

Anahita learnt from the webpage that the Tower of Silence was the holy place for the Parsi community that adhered to Zoroastrian faith. The Parsis believed that the earth and the fire were both holy and therefore, they did not bury or cremate their dead. Instead, they carried the dead and lay them to rest in the dakhmas.

Dākhma or the tower of silence was a circular structure where dead bodies were left for consumption by scavenging birds like the vulture. This tradition was called dokhmenashini. Parizaad was studying about the ancient tradition and making notes in that big brown book. Dokhmenashini makes sure that the dead bodies are left far away from human habitation at an elevated zone, where the rays of sun can decompose the dead bodies and scavenging birds can feed. The Parsis believed that the release of the human soul depended on that process. Many influential people like Dr Shariyar Parvez believed it was one of the best methods of saying the final farewell.

After learning everything, she searched for *Dakhma near me.* A second later, she had received the result, and startlingly, the nearest dakhma was just two minutes away from her house. It was a large green patch on the map. She rushed to the bedroom. It rained, and the moon peeped through gaps in the clouds.

She opened the glass door and inched towards the parapet, getting drenched in the rain with every step she took towards the edge. From there, she saw the world below – bright streetlamps, traffic signals, headlights and brake lights simmering in the company of rain drops. Just close to the hustle and bustle was the silence emanating from the green patch of land. She knew what was there: *The dakhma.*

When she turned, she saw the vulture perched on the sunshade, the bird's gaze penetrated Anahita's soul. Something flashed in front of her – a visual. The rainy night became a cloudy day, and in place of the vulture stood the woman in a maroon dress with a little girl behind her. It was a visual from the past that the ghost of Parizaad was showing her. Anahita's head exploded with a piercing pain. She heard the glass door slide. When she turned she saw a shadowy figure, thin and tall with soulless eyes. Anahita froze with fear.

44

～

Sheila Cooperative Society

THE TWO WOMEN HAD SPOILED FEROZIE'S DAY. HE HAD taken a long time to get over Parizaad, but the memories of the rebellious woman started haunting him that night. He skipped dinner and sat in front of the television – news as usual. One of the popular English news channels debated about the failure of the BMC at tackling flooding issues in the rainy season. Another one debated about the probability of a SARS-like pandemic from one of the wet markets in China.

'About a hundred people have shown flu-like symptoms in what appears to be caused by a previously unseen virus,' the Caucasian reporter in a PPE kit spoke while standing outside a hospital in China. 'Although the situation seems under control, the government has taken extra precautions to stop the spread of the novel virus. However, some experts in the White House believe that it might have been a leak from China's testing of a biological weapon …'

Stupid conspiracies! He switched to the next news channel, where they were reporting the recent metro shed deal and its impact on the environment. *This one looks interesting. Is it a political gimmick? Who is propelling the activism?*

As if in response, the news anchor introduced a well-groomed young man. 'Mr Abhinav Deshmukh, thank you for joining us. First of all, we would like to congratulate you for putting on such a great show today at the forest reserve area.'

Deshmukh? Ah! Must be the son of that Bhau. But wasn't he a bachelor? When did he have a son?

'Thank you!' the young Abhinav answered. He looked nothing less than a Bollywood actor, a finely groomed model in stylish Ray-Ban glasses. 'And thank you for having me here. It is an honour. I have grown up watching your news channel.'

'Well, *Nation Today* is the home of India's best journalists,' The anchor announced proudly before coming back to his questions for the young lad. 'Mr Abhinav, everything began with that tweet on your profile last night. Does it have anything to do with your uncle and his political agenda?'

Ferozie scoffed. *Uncle. The brat is his nephew! MNP wants to come back to power so badly.*

'Please don't link me with my *chachu*. I am an independent citizen concerned about my environment, about climate change. We have already made Mumbai one of the most polluted cities in the world and …'

Fuck off, propaganda! Ferozie frowned and switched off the television. He thought he would try to sleep reading a book in bed – *The Other Side of Her*. Outside, it started raining.

45

Nation Today Studio, Mahim

'I WANT TO CONVEY A SIMPLE MESSAGE TO THE PEOPLE IN power on behalf of the youth of Mumbai that our environment is dear to us. It is not some resting place for non-functioning metro rail compartments.' He paused for a moment and continued, 'Climate change experts have projected that anthropogenic climate change will swamp our city in less than thirty years. Unless we, the youth, take corrective action, the Arabian sea will siege the shore. Together with Guangzhou, Jakarta, and Miami, rising sea-levels from climate change has endangered *aamchi* Mumbai. Irregular rainfall and cyclones, scorching heat in the summers, and unbreathable air are all proof that inevitable doom is not some pseudoscientific prediction. It is happening now. Climate change is here, and what are we doing about it?' Abhinav glared at the camera, as if addressing the entire city, and said, 'We are just chopping down the lungs of the city.'

The news anchor said, 'But you know, Abhinav, the metro shed is very much a necessity for daily commuters. It will actually rid us of traffic congestions. If the Metro Rail Corp is to be believed, then the rise in levels of carbon dioxide due to tree felling in the forest will be compensated by roughly 197 trips within the first week of the Metro rail being fully functional. And one official tweeted that to construct something new, destruction becomes inevitable; but it also paves the way for new life and new creation. It will also provide employment for so many people.'

'And who is responsible for so much unemployment in the first place?' Abhinav shot back.

The anchor had arrived at the pre-decided question which would open the debate. 'The government says there is no alternative to the problem. Do you believe that?'

'There is an alternative.'

'What?'

'There is always an alternative, if you have the will to look for it.'

'Let our viewers know.'

'We can extend the existing railcoach sheds for Mumbai suburban trains in Andheri and Ghatkopar to accommodate metro coaches as well. There is a place on the western line. I know the infrastructure to connect the shed on ground with the metro rail will cost a lot but at least it will not destroy the green patch of reserved forest … *the lungs of the city*.' Abhinav looked directly at the camera. He had rehearsed well, and it was showing. 'We think that we got independence seventy-two years ago. Truth is, we are still enslaved. Enslaved by a corrupt government that only thinks about itself, not about its people. This corrupt government is not considering alternatives at all. It is because they don't want to. There are some dirty motives behind the transaction, and I will expose it too. You cannot fool the youth of Mumbai, CM *saahib*. We will set things right. Today, on the fifteenth of August, I am announcing a new movement to save Mumbai – a protest in the monsoon – a VARSHA-SATYAGRAHA! I invite everyone who cares for this city to join me tomorrow at the protest site – the proposed metro shed area.'

The other panellists, which also included Mehr, applauded Abhinav's eloquent words. Varun, who was sitting inside the VIP lounge, watched the telecast live on the television monitor in the room. He did not expect such a fine performance from the boy. He felt embarrassed for judging Abhinav based on that first meeting at Bhau's farmhouse a week ago. Abhinav's theatrics on national television raised Varun's confidence. He had it in his blood. He was a natural *actor* – an *abhineta*. An *abhineta* can easily become a *neta*.

Varun walked towards the monitor and stood in front of it. *When Bhau appears on television tomorrow and levels corruption charges on the incumbent chief minister, this boy will become a fan favourite, a youth icon!*

On the television, the anchor wrapped up the show, while Varun walked out of the studio with an unlit cigarette. He stood under the sunshade looking at the raindrops falling from the sky against the illumination of the streetlight. Varun felt relieved that moment, and just wanted to go home to fulfil his carnal desires. When was the last time he had had sex? Anahita was drunk that night, he remembered well. It was three months ago. The pinching allegations of Dr Shetty echoed in his ears.

She did it because she wanted a baby.

Varun stared at the cylindrical white cigarette. *Maybe I will just go home and jerk off; catch some sleep.* He accepted it as his fate.

'Varun?' Rekha's voice called from behind.

Varun turned and noticed the attractive woman.

'Need a light?' she asked politely eyeing the unlit cigarette in his hand. There was a glowing cigarette in hers.

'No, thank you. I am okay.'

'All right. By the way, Abhinav is extremely happy about the campaign. I guess they are all waiting for you in the VIP lounge.'

'Cool! I will join them shortly.'

'And …' Rekha hesitated.

'What is it, Rekha?'

'It's too late, and I am not comfortable taking a cab at this hour. Can you drop me home, Varun?' She came closer to him. The smell of tobacco from her lips worked like an aphrodisiac. Varun scanned the woman from head to toe. Inside his head, guilt and lust battled it out. He had held on for long, but he could not control it anymore. He finally said, 'Can I have the light?'

And for the first time in months, Varun broke his ritual and smoked.

46

~~

FEROZIE SNORED. THE TIPS OF HIS FINGER TOUCHED THE cover of the paperback even in his sleep. Raindrops splattered inside the house through the open window. Occasional thunder brightened up the vintage looking bedroom, modest by all means. Ferozie had switched off the night-lamp before dozing off.

Somebody opened the bedroom door and drifted towards him. The old man was unaware of the shadow drifting above him. The shadowy figure pulled out a cloth and a bottle of chloroform. It applied the sedative onto the cloth and then pressed the cloth against Ferozie's nostrils. He woke up briefly before he lost consciousness.

The figure carried the unconscious old man into the bathroom and turned on the tap, letting the water flow. Then, it went to the kitchen and returned with a boning knife. With the precision and patience of a cold-blooded killer, the figure sliced the old man's throat, severing the head from the rest of the body. Blood oozed out and streamed into the sink hole along with the running water. The figure washed its hand and the knife and closed the tap. It walked out of the bathroom with the knife, and then out of the house. After shutting the door, the figure placed a large lock on it.

Neighbours would suspect nothing. They would feel that the old man was away. Nobody would care even if he did not come back because the door was locked from the outside. Only the killer carried its key and the knowledge that Ferozie would never return.

47

·~·

Paradise Heights

Varun did not take his official car. He dismissed the driver as soon as their work at the studio was over. He caught up with Mehr, and she told him that Anahita was doing well. After making sure that Mehr had left, he booked an Uber for himself and Rekha. As they sat next to each other in the backseat, Varun glanced at Rekha. She looked irresistible. At her place, Rekha offered him a drink, and lust took over guilt and silenced it – at least for the night. *She lied to me about a baby.*

Later, Varun booked an Uber back to his apartment. At about 11.30 p.m., Varun arrived outside his apartment's gate. He walked in, and as usual, the watchman was not present. Varun spotted Keshav sleeping inside the car at the parking area as he walked towards their block.

Inside the elevator, there were muddy footprints all over the floor. Varun wondered if the maintenance folks were not cleaning it regularly during monsoon. When the doors of the elevator opened on the seventh floor, he noticed that the door to his apartment was ajar. Fresh muddy footprints connected the floor outside the elevator to the doorstep and it continued inside the living room until it reached the bathroom. His eyes nearly popped out of their sockets in shock when he saw someone lying unconscious under the tap. It was Anahita.

48

16 August 2019, Friday

Dr Shetty made an exception and agreed to see Anahita that morning before she left for the hospital. The reputed neuroscientist had received a call from the state health minister's office instructing her to take up Anahita's case on priority. She could not say no. When Varun had called her in the night after discovering his wife unconscious, the doctor asked him if Anahita had any wounds on her body. He noted that she had some bruises near the right ankle, but Anahita claimed that those happened in the morning. There weren't any other wounds on her body. The neuropsychiatrist asked Varun to calm down and bring her in the morning before the doctor left for work.

At the clinic, Dr Shetty checked Anahita's eyes with a flashlight. The pupils looked fine. 'What is the last thing that you remember before blacking out last night?'

'Um. I … I was reading something on the mobile. Then I went to the balcony.' Anahita struggled to recollect. 'I was looking at … at the dakhma.'

'*Dakhma*?' Dr Shetty turned off the flashlight.

'Yes, that is what I was reading about and when I read that there was one near my house, I came out to the balcony. It is visible from there. I mean, you can't see the tower or anything, but you can see the thick wooded area.'

'All right.' The doctor placed the flashlight on her table and started walking back to her chair. 'What did you see or hear right before the blackout?'

'I … ' Anahita pushed harder into her memories. Some images flashed before her, but nothing connected. She closed her eyes for a moment and then said, 'There was someone else. I felt like it came after me. So, I ran inside … I can't remember anything else.'

'Did you go outside before you had this episode?' Dr Shetty got ready to jot down her notes in Anahita's patient record. 'Did you leave the building's premises?'

'I … I am not sure. I definitely didn't go outside before reading the book. It was raining heavily.' Anahita said. She looked at her husband twice, wondering if he had already declared her insane in his mind.

'Well, I think your dissociated personality is trying to show up more frequently. You should be more careful. I have to monitor you.'

'What's causing this, Dr Shetty?' Varun who had been quietly observing, asked.

'Like I told you in my diagnosis, her right amygdala is damaged. But the splitting and time loss has nothing to do with the amygdala. I need to dig out what's going on in her subconscious mind. Maybe there are suppressed memories or repressed episodes from the past.' Dr Shetty glanced at Anahita and asked, 'You said you had an accident in your childhood. Right?'

'Yes, doctor. I was seven years old.'

'How vividly do you remember being in the accident?'

'I was crossing the road with my mother at a signal. It was red. A motorbike came racing from the opposite side, breaking the signal, and hit me.'

'Can you picture it vividly?'

'Well, I am not sure.'

'And you were hit on the head.'

'Yes.'

'What else do you remember from your childhood.'

'Not much, just whatever my mother told me. It has been foggy since that accident.'

'You mean, memories prior to that accident are blurry?'

'Yes, exactly.'

'So you have formed some vague visuals based on what your mother has told you, but they appear as bits and pieces, mostly unclear?'

'What are you saying, doc?' Varun asked, concerned.

The neuropsychiatrist removed her glasses and sat back on her chair, looking at Anahita's nervous face. 'Dr Malhotra mentioned nothing about retrograde amnesia in her report. But it is clear from what you just said that you have retrograde amnesia prior to the accident. You have successfully formed memories after the accident, but everything before that is a complete blank – *Tabula Rasa*.'

There was a moment of silence in the room. Anahita tried to picture events from her life before the accident. She realized she didn't even have a real memory of the accident.

'Why don't you come in the evening, after nine? I would like to schedule a hypnotherapy session with you.'

'Sure, if it helps.'

'I think it would. I think the root cause of all your issues lies there, and I will try to pull that out.'

'All right, we will see you in the evening,' Varun said, and the husband and wife left the clinic.

There was silence in the car. Since Varun was present, Keshav did not play any music. Anahita looked out of the window, sitting alone in the back. She did not look tense. In fact, she seemed at ease. Varun's mind was in turmoil because his guilt had taken over again. He was with his secretary last night, when he could have come home and prevented his wife from putting her life at risk. Besides, Bhau kept calling. The big man was going to appear on television later in the day, but Varun's content team hadn't delivered the script because they were waiting for Varun's approval. Whatever happened the previous night unsettled his mind. So, he planned to go through the 2000-word script once he was in the office. The thought of leaving Anahita alone, especially when Keshav failed to keep a check on her the previous night, scared him. Varun vented his frustration on the driver. 'Where were you, Keshav, when madam went outside?' Varun asked.

The question surprised the driver. 'I was down only. I did not see her coming out even once. I think it was the ghost.'

Varun's anger bolstered at the driver's excuse. 'You were asked to look after her and instead you were sleeping in the car.'

'I … I was not sleeping. I was awake till you came.'

'Yeah, right! I was the one who was sleeping.'

'I am sorry, sir. I will be more careful from today. Please do not complain to Bhau.'

Varun ignored the plea and turned towards Anahita, who was sitting in the seat behind him. 'I had told you to come to the studio with Mehr. Why did you have to go back home and stay all alone?'

'I … I wanted to rest, Varun.'

'You could have rested at the studio and avoided all of this.' Varun included his sexual escapade among *all of this*. 'Whatever! I am fed up of everything.'

'What is wrong with you, Varun? I told you I will manage this.'

'Yeah, right, you do that. Either you go back to Gurugram or I am going to ask your mother to come and babysit you. I cannot concentrate on work because of you.' The words came out like razor blades.

'Of course, your career, that is all that you have ever cared about.'

'I am doing this for you as well as for the *secret* baby that you are carrying.'

'Nice to know that, Varun. I am so grateful to you.' Sarcasm was unlike Anahita, but in that moment, her anger consumed her – anger at her husband's complete lack of empathy. 'Look, Varun, I am having a tough time right now. It would be good if you stopped being a jerk for once in our *extremely happy* married life. I understand your pressures and I don't want you to be bothered about me. I will go back to Gurugram as soon as I find answers to my questions.'

'There you go again! There are no questions, Anahita. It is all in your mind. It is your fucking imagination.'

'I thought so too. But I know there is something more looming in that dakhma.'

'I hope Dr Shetty can dig out the truth from your mind tonight and put an end to your stupid quest.' Varun looked away. 'Keshav, could you please drop me at the office and then take madam home?'

'Of course, sir.'

Varun and Anahita did not speak after that. Keshav had to tolerate the uncomfortable silence that prevailed until they reached their destination.

Anahita took out her phone and looked up *Tabula Rasa*. A page on the Britannica website read:

Comparison of the mind to a blank writing tablet occurs in Aristotle's De anima, and the Stoics and the Peripatetics subsequently argued for an original state of mental blankness (at the time of birth). Both the Aristotelians and the Stoics, however, emphasized those faculties of the mind or soul that, having been only potential or inactive before receiving ideas from the senses, respond to the ideas by an intellectual process and convert them into knowledge.

The English empiricist John Locke, in An Essay Concerning Human Understanding *(1689), argued for the mind's initial resemblance to 'white paper, a blank slate, void of all characters,' with 'all the materials of reason and knowledge' derived from experience.*

Anahita stopped reading and let the information sink in. The info on the internet referred to the brain devoid of any memories at the time of birth. She quickly searched for the etymology of the term.

> *Tabula rasa is a Latin phrase often translated as 'clean slate' in English and originates from the Roman tabula used for notes, which was blanked by heating the wax and then smoothing it. This roughly equates to the English term 'blank slate' (or, more literally, 'erased slate') which refers to the emptiness of a slate prior to it being written on with chalk. Both may be renewed repeatedly, by melting the wax of the tablet or by erasing the chalk on the slate.*

Chalk on slate – on blackboard. That was Anahita's mind after the accident. She had no recollection of what happened before her accident in 1999. All the memories and knowledge of seven years since her birth had been erased, like the contents on a slate, rubbed off like the diagram on a blackboard. *Tabula Rasa.*

But sometimes, bits of chalk dust still stick on to the blackboard, like afterimages that made no sense, unless you can retrieve the erased memories.

In Anahita's view, the phone's screen transformed into a miniature blackboard, and on them was the alveolar sac diagram. She could see the diagram appearing, bringing scary memories from the past. Her heart raced.

She closed her eyes tightly.

Breathe in. Breathe out. Everything is not *under our control.*

49

The Indie, Versova

MEHR STOOD OUTSIDE HER OFFICE GATE WITH A THIN Verve cigarette in her hand. Many smokers who could not quit cigarettes switched over to such thinner rolls believing they would consume less tobacco with every drag. This was not true, and Mehr knew that. Yet she stood there on the side of the road blowing rings of smoke into the breezy air of the seaside locality. Two things brewed tangentially in her mind – the interview with Bhau on *Nation First* that evening and the mysterious chain of events that started with Anahita's delusions. A black sedan pulled up on the road, right behind her. The back door opened, and a tall man emerged from the car. The man they had seen outside the fire temple. But what was he doing there?

'Ms Mehrab Hussain?'

'Yes?'

'I am Nariman.'

'Hi, Nariman. I saw you with Ferozie the other day. What do you want?'

'Shall we go to a more private place to converse?'

'All right. We can talk in my office.'

Once the two were settled in Mehr's office, Nariman came straight to the point, 'Why are you inquiring about that woman?'

'You mean Parizaad?'

Nariman did not respond, but it was evident from the look on his face that he was referring to the same person as *the woman*.

'It is my friend, Anahita. She is living in the same apartment where Parizaad had committed suicide allegedly after killing her daughter. I have known Anahita since third standard. Her mind was never stable, it was vulnerable. So, when she moved to that house, she started seeing the ghost of Parizaad.'

'Ghost?'

'Yes! That is what she believes. Although her psychiatrist, husband, and I dismiss it completely. At least, I did, but then she told me she dreamt of a dead vulture. She said that the ghost of Parizaad begged for help in her dream. As a friend, I supported her thought and helped her investigate. However, it led me to your old guy.' She looked at Nariman and stressed on the name '*Ferozie*. Coincidentally, Anahita had fainted few days ago in front of his house with no memory of being there. Ferozie had seen her too. He recognized her when we went to see him yesterday. But then his tone changed when we mentioned Parizaad. It was like her name touched a nerve. I was sure that he knew something. As a journalist, my instincts told me to follow him. I did and arrived at Agiyari lane. I saw you there. And now you are here.'

The tall man sighed.

Mehr leaned forward on the chair, placed her arms over the desk in front of her and inquired, 'Who was Parizaad?'

'You are a journalist. Your words can do a lot of damage.'

'I promise you. I just want to find out about Parizaad to help my friend. Day by day, she is losing her grip on reality.'

'Do you believe in God, Ms Hussain?'

'No.'

'I appreciate your honesty, Ms Hussain.'

'Thank you.'

'Promise me you will not ask questions after listening to what I have to say.'

'I promise.'

50

N ARIMAN CLEARED HIS THROAT AND BEGAN:
'Parizaad was a free-spirited girl. I had known her
since she was a child. She was born in a Hindu family but
her parents passed away in an accident. The little baby didn't
even have a name when Homyar found her on the streets.
Homyar raised her as his own, named her Parizaad. Homyar,
his wife and son were very fond of Parizaad. She was smart
and excelled in academics. But changed when she started
going to college. She discovered love. Every time she saw the
boy who stood up for revloutionary reforms, she would feel a
piece of her heart dissipating, like petals in the wind. She was
in love, and he was her lover. He was very active in college
politics and she'd go to any extent to support him. This boy …
he was an atheist, and eventually, Parizaad was influenced by
his ideas. And then one day, she got pregnant with his child.

'The news reached her brother, and eventually everyone in
the neighbourhood knew about it. Neighbours and friends
blamed Homyar for giving her too much freedom. There was
a lot of pressure on Parizaad, and she was close to having
a mental breakdown. However, before that could happen,

Parizaad eloped with her lover. They went to Delhi. They had the child together. However, the lover did not stay with her for long after. He returned to Mumbai, for his true ambitions were calling him. He promised to marry her as soon as his political career stabilized. She believed him. He would go to see her occasionally at first, but soon, he stopped visiting. Tired of waiting, Parizaad came back to Mumbai with her child. While Parizaad was depressed of waiting, her lover was soaring like a lion on the political stage. He juggled his revolutionary ideologies with regionalism and nationalism, as and when required. The lover could not risk his ambitions by accepting the fact that he had a seven-year-old daughter before marriage. It would shatter his reputation and jeopardize his future. He asked Parizaad to give him some more time, and she moved into that apartment in Paradise Heights.

'A week later, she learnt that Homyar had passed away. She arrived late and could not see the last rites. She waited outside the dakhma holding on to her tears, and cried only after coming back home. From the balcony of her apartment, she watched the clouds mourning above the dakhma's estate. Alas, there was not a single vulture in the sky.'

Nariman paused. He shifted uncomfortably in his seat and then spoke again. 'Ms Hussain, the story until here is believable. Now, you must take a leap of faith with me, for Parizaad was no ordinary woman.'

Mehr nodded.

Nariman continued, 'On the third night after Homyar's death, a voice woke Parizaad up. The voice of Homyar. She shuddered at first but then gathered courage to look out of the glass door. She saw the undead form of Homyar at the balcony, begging for help. At first, she did not understand what was going on, but she started seeing Homyar wherever she went – always begging for help. She thought she was hallucinating. She went to a doctor who diagnosed the onset of schizophrenia. And then she started seeing a vulture in her dreams. She had a dream in which a vulture crashed in front of her, but when she went near it, a hand came out of the ground and grabbed her foot. She contacted her brother, but he turned her away. And then she contacted me.

'I listened to her. I realized she was not asking for help. She actually had a delusional theory and wanted to do something about it. She believed that the decline in the number of vultures was affecting Dokhmenashini. *Some departing souls in the dākhma did not ascend to the after-life*, she claimed. Such a claim came when the community was already reeling under the debate whether bodies should be cremated in the absence of vultures. The people thought she was part of the group that was pushing for cremation. But cremation is not the natural way of crossing over. For us, fire is holy and so is the earth, so we place the dead in the dākhma, for the vultures to feed. But when there were no vultures, what could we do?

'I couldn't help her but promised to keep her story a secret. Parizaad started digging stuff up. She had already made some friends in the media. Some activists who were protesting at the decline of the vulture population in India also supported her, although her quest differed from theirs. Parizaad was convinced that the decline of vultures was the reason Homyar's soul did not ascend to heaven.

'There were speculations at the time that rapid construction and corruption in the ministry was partly responsible for the extinction of vultures in the region. She followed the theory and traced the people responsible for the decline. Those in power labelled her a conspirator against the government.

They suppressed her voice and the voice of the environmental activists. But Parizaad was not going to give up. She started a movement to recruit young ones who cared for the environment. Rumours of her schizophrenia floated among people. They said she was mentally ill and depressed because of her failed love.

'And then it happened. She gave up her life one night. It did not make it to the news though, as if someone did not want it there.' Nariman sighed. 'That is all I know about Parizaad.'

After listening to Nariman, Mehr felt sorry for Parizaad. What the woman had to go through was the fate of almost any woman in the world who dared to follow her heart. She had many questions.

'I don't believe she would take her life like a coward,' Mehr said.

'I don't know. Yes, she was strong. She gave a good fight back then, but perhaps it was her hallucinations. She strongly believed that the ghost she saw was real.'

'Just like Anahita. She also believes that Parizaad's ghost is real. She had also seen a vulture in her dream. Yeah, a hand grabbed her foot too. Anahita heard Parizaad calling out for help.'

'Well, Parizaad had a reason to hallucinate about Homyar – he raised her like a father. But I don't understand why your friend would see Parizaad. She has no connection with the woman who committed suicide twenty years ago.' Nariman added, 'Perhaps she read something about it. Did you know a writer has written some story based on the suicide?'

'You mean that Tejwani guy?'

'I think so. It became a topic of controversy when he published the story in his book. But what he has written in the story has nothing to do with reality at all. In fact, it was far-fetched and stupid. He claimed Parizaad was part of some Satanic cult, which has no element of truth in it. I give you my word.'

'What was the connection between Parizaad and Ferozie?'

Nariman sighed. 'Ferozie was Homyar's son. Ferozie and Parizaad shared a bond that even real siblings do not.'

'Do you think he had something to do with her suicide?'

'Never! There is not a single day he doesn't mourn his sister's decision.'

'What about the lover?'

'Ms Hussain, you had promised me you won't ask questions at the end. But it seems you have forgotten your promise. Now, I'd like to take your leave.'

'Please, tell me if you know who it is.'

'Only Homyar knew. Parizaad never disclosed the identity of her lover to anyone else. Not even Ferozie.'

'Do you think it could be a murder?'

'I dislike speculating … especially about the dead, Ms Hussain. It doesn't give me any pleasure. But murder is a sin, and if anyone has sinned, then they will be brought to justice by the will of God, with the help of yazatas who are looking after us.' Nariman got up.

'I don't believe in God or in divine powers.'

'Yes, of course.' Nariman smiled. He thought for a moment and then added, 'You know, Ms Hussain, your friend reminds me of a female *yazata* … an angel that personifies water.'

'What?'

'In her hymn, she is invoked as the wide-expanding, healing, righteous foe of the tyrant *daevas*. She purifies seeds of men and wombs of women, gives strength to mothers.

She is the strong one among the angels. Whenever there is injustice, like the splashing waters of a violent rain, she'll torment the tyrant *daevas* and bring them to justice,' Nariman said and started walking towards the door.

'What does this angel have to do with my friend?' Mehr asked politely.

'Her name means moist, strong and pure. Do you know what this yazata is called, Ms Hussain?'

'No … ' Mehr was clueless about the intricacies of the Zoroastrian religion. She didn't know the name of the *yazata*.

Nariman smiled, a twinkle in his eye, and said, '*Aredvi Sura … Anahita.*'

Mehr thought about Parizaad and the injustice done to her by the man she loved. She thought about the child she bore. *Aredvi Sura Anahita*, the angel of strength. Maybe the dead woman's spirit was asking for Anahita's help. Mehr's rational mind couldn't quite believe it. However, the connections were getting stronger, and she wanted to arrive at the truth. She decided to call one of her sources in Delhi to dig up information, before heading to the interview with Bhau.

51

According to Varun's plan, Bhau's interview on live television would start the prime-time debate. However, Bhau refused to go live. He had had a terrible experience once with a veteran journalist. Although the news editor had provided a list of questions that the journalist would ask during the live telecast, the journo went off script and asked questions on corruption within Bhau's cabinet and his own perusal of communal identity-based politics. Bhau stuttered and stammered, something the people had never seen before. Eventually, he lost the following election. He had to form a coalition government, but the coalition leader changed his mind and ditched Bhau. He had not been in power since. That was also one of the reasons why he did not want to come back as the CM candidate. He knew that the opposition would tear him apart.

On her way to the studio, Mehr called up her friend, Satbir, an investigative journalist from New Delhi.

'Can you do me a favour, Satbir?'

'As long as you don't ask me to resign and join *The Indie. Yahan achi salary mil jaati hain.*' Satbir had a thick Punjabi accent.

Mehr laughed. 'Hey, I was planning to make you head of my Delhi wing.'

'Aji haan. Anyway, tell me what favour do you want from me?'

'I want some details about a woman called Parizaad.'

'Parizaad?'

'Yeah! This would be from' – she calculated in her mind – 'the 1990s. She had moved from Mumbai and given birth to a girl.'

'And?'

'And that is all I know. Need to find out in which hospital she gave birth to the child. I need the hospital records – her address, the father's name, doctor … anything at all.'

'You want me to find out about a woman just by her name. Are you serious?'

'Yes! You are the only one who can do it.'

There was brief pause on the line, and Mehr could hear the typical sound of Delhi traffic, with echoes of someone yelling in Haryanvi.

'Give me some time. Okay? I will get what you need. I have a guy who can get through to hospitals. I will call you as soon as I get something.'

'How much time? It's urgent.'

'In this age of WhatsApp and 4G, it won't take that long.'

'All right. Thanks, Satbir.'

After disconnecting the call, Mehr saw an email from Varun's team – a list of questions she would ask Bhau in a few minutes from then. She looked at them. Very smooth and conveniently structured to give Bhau the upper hand.

Varun, you son of a gun!

Her cab honked its way through the traffic. Thanks to the water-logging, the vehicles hardly seemed to move on the road. It had been raining continuously for thirty-six hours.

52

‘Y ES, IT IS GOING WELL. THE TWITTER CAMPAIGN WAS superb. Abhinav has received a lot of support at the *varshasatyagraha* today, despite the non-stop rain. Bhau's interview will catapult him as the talking point on every news channel and WhatsApp group,' Varun conveyed looking at the video stream of Desai on his laptop's screen.

'Excellent!' Desai smiled. An expression of concern came over his face as he asked, 'How is your wife? Better?'

'Not really. She had another episode last night. Nothing bad happened though.'

'Thank God. Did you take her to the doctor?'

'Yes. In fact, when you called in the morning, I was at the doctor's place. She has asked her to come for a hypnotherapy session.'

'Hypnosis? I hope the doctor knows what she is doing. Hypnosis is no joke. Beta, you can take the load off your shoulder. I genuinely feel that right now you should be with your wife.'

'I'll manage, Mr Desai.'

'Did you talk to Deshmukh?'

'Yes.'

'What did he say?'

'He has offered his support but wants me to stay till the end. He's thrilled by the initial response of the campaign.'

After a brief pause, Desai said, 'You know what? I'm coming to Mumbai. I'll talk to Deshmukh in person and make him understand.'

'I don't want you to take that trouble for me.'

'Oh please, Varun. I can do that for you. Besides, Mumbai is my second home. It's been long since I have visited my brother who lives there. I'd also make sure that I see your wife. If there is anything that you can learn from me, son, is that those who love you are more important than anything else in this world.'

'Thanks, Mr Desai. You know, my dad passed away when I was three. I don't even remember seeing him, except in photographs. Sometimes, I feel you truly are the father I never had,' Varun said with a tear in his eye.

'Destiny has its own way of bringing people together, son. Stay strong!'

A technician nudged Varun. 'Sir? Varun Sir?'

Varun muted the Skype call and turned around. 'What is it?'

'We're ready. Bhau wants you there.'

'All right, I'm coming.'

Varun unmuted the Skype and spoke to Desai, 'Well, I have to go now. I will see you soon.'

'Take care, Varun.'

Varun closed his laptop and rushed to the programming area, where Bhau was waiting. Mehr had also arrived.

53

7E, Paradise Apartments

AFTER COMING BACK HOME FROM DR SHETTY'S CLINIC, Anahita lay down on her bed but could not sleep. The images from the book flashed before her eyes. The cries of help from the dead woman in the dream reverberated in her mind. She spoke to her mother on the phone for some time. The conversation helped calm her. Shortly after, she received a call from Mehr, who was on her way to the studio. Mehr had learnt a lot about Parizaad through someone called Nariman and promised to tell Anahita everything in the evening, but Anahita did not have the patience to wait that long. She decided to meet Mehr at the studio.

A few minutes later, Keshav pulled out the car from the parking and drove Anahita to the studio. Keshav enjoyed driving in the rain with his music. The car entered the NS Patkar Marg. To the left, Anahita saw the elevated area beyond which the dakhma was located.

'Keshav?' she called the driver.

'Yes, madam? You don't like the music? I will change.'

'No. No. The music is fine. I wanted to know what's there.' She pointed at the area.

The driver followed Anahita's finger. 'Oh. That is a park. You can climb the stairs to get there. There is also some Parsi holy place.'

'Can you take me there?'

'Madam, I just crossed the exit road. Now, I will have to take a U-turn and drive all the way back.'

'Please do that.'

'Sure, madam. I will take you there.'

The Doongerwadi in the lush green area on the eastern side of Malabar Hill had many towers of silence or dakhmas. The early occupants built the first dakhma there in 1670, as it was far away from the city. However, over time, more towers were constructed there; meanwhile, the metropolitan city conquered all areas around the Doongerwadi.

When Anahita arrived at the entrance gate, she was startled because the place looked exactly as it had in her dream, except in the dream, she had been on the other side of the gate. It was eerily silent. The wall was high, and she could only see the tiled roofs of some quarters inside. She knocked on the gate and soon she heard someone coming.

'What do you want?' a man wearing a white dress answered from inside. It was a *khandia*. He had grown morose with age. Khandias were corpse bearers designated to handle the dead remains of people. They carried the bodies only up till the dakhmas, and thereafter, another type of corpse-bearers called *nassasalars* took the bodies inside.

'I … I want to come in.'

'You cannot come inside. This is a restricted area. Are you Parsi?'

'No, I'm not.' Anahita thought for a moment and then asked, 'But can you tell me if you know something about Parizaad?' It was a shot in the dark.

There was momentary silence. Then the man came forward and stood right in front of Anahita, with the gate separating them, and said, 'No, madam.'

'Oh, ok. Thank you.'

Anahita sighed. She looked at the serene entrance one more time and then started walking back to the car. She realized the futility of her exercise.

Meanwhile, Keshav was updating Bhau through WhatsApp about Anahita's new area of interest – the dakhma.

54

THE FIRST HALF OF THE INTERVIEW WENT ON FOR almost ninety minutes. The producer called for a long break. Bhau went back to the VIP lounge with Varun and Rekha. When Bhau opened his phone, he saw Keshav's message on WhatsApp.

'Madam is in doongerwadi dakhma.'

The message was followed by a picture of the woman talking at the gate. Bhau was disturbed by the message. Varun also noticed the sudden change in the politician's face.

'What is wrong, Bhau?'

'Your wife is really unwell. Isn't she?' Bhau asked. Before Varun could answer, Bhau added, 'Otherwise, why would she go to a dakhma?' He showed the picture to Varun.

'How did you get this picture?'

'I had asked Keshav to monitor your wife. Just in case. But this is weird, Varun …'

'It is that house and that woman she keeps talking about.' Varun sounded frustrated.

'I can understand. We will talk about this later. Let me finish this interview first. Keshav is bringing her to the studio now.'

'Okay. Thank you, Bhau, for taking care of her. I really appreciate you taking the pain to monitor her. I should be the one doing it.'

Bhau nodded at Varun and returned to the set. He had to finish the remaining part of his interview with Mehr before getting involved in this new mess that Varun's wife had embraced.

<hr>

During the break, Mehr tried to get in touch with her colleague, Satbir. He had dropped a message asking her to call him. After two unsuccessful attempts, Satbir finally answered the third call.

'Hi. I saw your message.' Mehr was eager to know if there was a breakthrough.

'Mehr, I guess this is your lucky day because my guy did not have to make too many calls.'

'Tell me about her.'

'This woman gave birth in a private hospital in Chhatarpur.'

'Are you sure?'

'I could be wrong, but my guy could not find any other person by that name and year in the records of over fifty hospitals in the region. Everything is digitized, so it does not take much time to search for a name. It cost me some money, but I contacted the hospital and got the file out. I am sending them to you. There is no name listed as the husband or the child's father. But there was something useful in the consent form.'

'Consent form?'

'Yes, apparently, the woman's delivery was a C-section. The hospital had taken a consent form from the partner before performing the surgery, because there were some other complications.'

'And?' Mehr asked, increasingly impatient to get to the bottom of things.

' … and here is the interesting thing. Wait. I will not tell you this and spoil it. Just check your WhatsApp, the last image. At the end, you will find a signature.'

Mehr pulled the phone from her ear, put the call on speaker and minimized the dialler-screen. She pressed on the latest WhatsApp notification from Satbir. An image opened. She pinched the bottom part to zoom into the image. She noted the signature, a familiar one.

'Did you see?'

It took a second for Mehr to realize whose signature it was. 'No way!'

'Yes, it is him – the one and only!'

'This is huge, Satbir. I will talk to you later.' Mehr disconnected the call, put the phone inside her pocket, and rushed inside. She had an interview to complete – one that could now stray from the script she was given.

55

Commissioner Godbole had a special dislike for the incumbent chief minister. He had voted for Bhau in the last election, and the one before that. Godbole had been with Bhau from the time the latter entered college politics. After college, Godbole had a tough time battling communal discrimination, and it was Bhau who got him in the police force. When the coalition fell apart after the last election results, Godbole, just like Bhau's other supporters, came to know that their leader would not be forming the government in the state anymore. There was widespread angst among the voters who felt cheated by the ruling party. Indeed, democracy was nothing but demagoguery by the people, for the people and of the people (in that order). People like Godbole were ready to sacrifice their life for Bhau. So when he got a call from Bhau asking him to check a particular house in Crawford Market, he immediately obeyed.

When he arrived at the old house in Sheila Cooperative Society, the large lock on the door welcomed him. The neighbours were clueless as to where the old man who lived in the house had gone. They found it unusual, for Ferozie hadn't left the house like that in a long time. One neighbour even claimed that the lock used on the door did not belong to Ferozie. Bhau had asked Godbole to knock down the door if required, and he did so. A pungent smell filled the air inside the small house.

The odour originated from the bathroom and what the police officers witnessed there was a sight of overwhelming gore. Immediately, the news reached all media outlets, and it went something like this: *A resident reported that the old man had disappeared and a rotting odour came from his house. The police arrived at the scene. When they broke open the house, they found that the man's head had been severed from the body, and it was lying in the bathroom.*

The resident who gave the statement was also a die-hard Bhau loyalist – a nexus set up by Bhau and Godbole. News channels ran the story of a gruesome murder on the ticker while covering Abhinav's *Varshasatyagrah*. The movement was gaining support from the youth of the city. The name was coined by Varun; however, he knew nothing about the murders yet.

56

Nation Today Studio

BHAU ANSWERED ALL THE QUESTIONS DIPLOMATICALLY. Each word that came out of his mouth immunized Abhinav, before the nephew bungee jumped into the political arena. Mehr looked vigilantly at the ex-chief minister of the state. She had something against him but could not use it in public, not so soon. Bhau was too powerful to be taken down with weak evidence. She waited for the interview to get over, and then she would ask the important questions in private. She had finally arrived at the last question on the list Varun's content team had given her. Anahita had also reached the studio. Mehr could see her timid friend standing next to Varun, far behind the production crew.

'Bhau, my last question to you tonight is something that everyone has in their minds. What is the future of your party? Will Abhinav be the face of a new era?' Mehr asked, feeling more forced than ever.

'While growing up, Abhinav focused on his education. Unlike me, he is a post-graduate from one of the world's top business schools. We never exposed him to politics. But he always had this deep concern for the environment. I still remember, when I had visited Versova beach for an event, this was many years ago, while everyone was hooked to my speech, Abhinav, who was just six or seven years old, was plucking plastic waste that people had thrown there. This inspired some young activists to carry out drives later.' The minister's made-up story took credit away from the volunteers who had actually started the movement.

Bhau continued, 'So, he has always had this genuine concern for nature. Abhi is a pure vegetarian because he cannot see animals getting hurt, and I support him. He's there to make a difference. A soldier of mother nature. He is not there to do politics. But …' Bhau changed his tone, 'there is politics involved in the metro-shed deal. We'll expose that in due time and, in the process, if Abhinav ends up in politics then I assure you he will be a much more aware and responsible politician than all of us oldies put together. Our generation of politicians focused on economic development only because the middle-class of the nineties wanted a better standard of living, better salaries. But Abhinav's generation knows that without a clean safe environment, you can't live at all. He'll be a woke *neta*.' The old politician smiled with a sparkle in his eye.

What a performance! Mehr thought. Out loud, she said, 'We are all looking forward to that. Thank you so much, Bhau, for giving us your valuable time.' She extended her hand.

Bhau did a *namaste* instead. 'Thank you very much.'

After the interview, the politician walked to the VIP lounge. Varun followed. Mehr removed her wires and called Anahita. First, she took a printout of the consent form that Satbir had sent her. Anahita was clueless. They also headed to the VIP lounge.

Varun was discussing the next phase of the plan with Bhau when Anahita and Mehr entered the room.

'Bhau?' Mehr called out. 'I need to know a few things … off record.' She had the print out in her hand.

'Mehr, can this wait? We are in the middle of an important discussion,' Varun objected.

'No!' Mehr sounded stern.

Bhau silenced Varun with a gesture. 'Go on, Mehr.'

Mehr looked dead straight into Bhau's eyes and said, 'Tell us about your successor.'

'Well, don't you know about him already? I just gave you a whole interview about Abhinav.'

'No, the other successor you don't talk about.'

'What do you mean?'

'Tell me … how are you linked with the woman called Parizaad.'

An expression of discomfort appeared on Bhau's withered face. The question also surprised Anahita. Why was Mehr asking Bhau about Parizaad?

Varun interrupted, irritated by the name of the woman, 'First it was my wife. Now you too have contracted her madness? Is this *folie à deux*?'

'Varun, I didn't ask you. The question was for Bhau.' Mehr kept her gaze fixed on the politician.

Bhau reached for the bottled water on the table. 'I don't know any Parizaad. Who is that?'

'Really? Then why did you sign on her consent form twenty-seven years ago?' Mehr handed the printout to Bhau. 'Isn't that your signature, Mr Dayanand Deshmukh?'

By now, it was evident to everyone that Bhau was raging inside. The vein on his forehead throbbed with fury. The seasoned politician grabbed the printed paper and stood up. He marched towards Mehr and through clenched teeth said, 'Don't you dare … otherwise … ' He crumpled the paper and threw it into the waste bin in the corner of the room.

Bhau shoved the woman aside and walked out of the room. Anahita looked on in shock. Varun ran after the politician, trying to pacify him.

'What is going on, Mehr?' asked Anahita, confused by the turn of events.

'I will tell you everything on the way home. Come!' Mehr took Anahita's hand and walked out of the room.

～

Bhau's car waited for him at the studio's gate. He grabbed the door and was about to open it when Varun called out from behind. 'Bhau, I'm so sorry about all this.'

Bhau turned around and grumbled, 'Look, I'll say this only once. If your wife doesn't stop this madness, then I will take care of things in my way … and trust me, you won't live to see it.'

Bhau then got inside his car and it zoomed out of the gate. Once inside, he dialled a number. Some rings later, a shrill voice answered, 'Yes, what happened now?'

Bhau barked into the phone. 'That journalist is going to fuck us.'

Silence for a few seconds and then the slithery voice replied, 'I had already told you what to do.'

'Yes, it's done. Godbole is on it. They'll find the other two bodies as well. Tomorrow, the city will talk about a new serial killer and our news channels will accuse this crazy woman of the crime. Like you said, I will also get that doctor … Shetty … to testify about Anahita's mental condition. But what to do about this Mehrab Hussain?'

'How much does she know?'

'The bitch knows.' He whispered, 'She brought the hospital forms. I'll find out who her source was.'

'Then tomorrow is too late. What has to be done must be done now.'

'You mean …'

'Yes, do it!' the voice hissed. 'And don't forget to take care of Keshav as well. We do not need his services anymore. Whatever is left, I will take care of it. There is a reason they called me *the scavenger*.'

'Because you clean up rot.'

A chuckle from the other end. Bhau disconnected the call and then dialled Godbole.

57

DESPITE THE LASHING RAINFALL, KESHAV SWIFTLY drove the car onto the highway. Water had stagnated on the sides and it was worse in the pocket roads. That was the situation every year during the monsoon months in Mumbai. But the temperaments of the passengers inside his car were, in that moment, much worse than the city's streets had ever been.

Varun exploded at Mehr and Anahita. 'I asked for your support because the doctor thought your involvement might help improve Anahita's condition. Instead, you got behind her frenzy and pushed her deeper into this abyss? What the fuck is wrong with you?'

'Oh, is it my fault? I was only trying to help Anahita. If you had been even a tad more supportive in the beginning, she would have not lost it in the first place. You know that, right?'

'Please stop it, you guys!' Anahita cried, a hand on her belly. 'I am not feeling well.'

'What happened?'

'I'm queasy.'

'Keshav, can you please pull over after that petrol pump? There is an Udupi restaurant there. The owner is a friend; he will let us use the restroom.'

'Okay, madam.'

Varun and Keshav waited in the car. Mehr accompanied Anahita to the hotel. Like most of the Udupi vegetarian hotels in Mumbai, migrants from Mangalore ran it. Mayank Salian was one. He was a friend from Mehr's modelling days. Neither made it as models, but they made it in life.

As Mehr chatted with her old buddy, Anahita waddled inside the women's restroom. She threw up in the sink. Her eyes watered with each heave until she was done.

When Anahita came out of the bathroom, Mehr hurried over to her side. 'Are you okay now?'

'I guess so,' replied Anahita. 'My head feels lighter, and tummy is ticklish. I don't know how to describe it, Mehr.'

'Don't worry. Just don't think about all of this. I will sit with Varun and try to work this out. Avoid the stress. All right?'

'I'll try.'

'Let's go.' Mehr glanced at her friend at the cash counter. 'Thanks, Mayank. I will catch up with you later. Bye!'

When Anahita and Mehr came out of the restaurant, the Innova was still on the road. A distance of hundred meters and a few thousand raindrops separated them from the

Innova's door. Anahita could see Varun waving out from the car, asking them to come quickly.

That was the last thing Anahita saw, before a truck came crashing into the parked car, sending it rolling into the petrol pump on the other side of the road. The truck sped away. The Innova went tumbling into a petrol dispenser, like a piece of scrap metal. An explosion followed.

At that moment, a deafening silence rang in Anahita's ears. The balls of fire that swivelled out of the explosion spiralled into the shape of little fiery black smoke sacks – alveoli sacs. Later, that would be all Anahita could recall.

58

11 July 2010, Saturday
Mumbai

'MOM HAS GROWN SUSPICIOUS ABOUT US, MEHR.' Anahita said, curled up on the bed, her back towards her friend. 'She has asked me to come back to Gurugram.'

Mehr tried to pull her around, but Anahita would not budge. She sighed as she placed her right arm over Anahita's shoulder. 'You aren't her slave, Anahita. You are the master of your life. Listen to your heart, and do as it says.'

'I can't hurt my mom.'

'So, you're choosing to let the train run over you? Is that it?'

'She said that this is not natural – whatever we have between us.' Tears filled Anahita's eyes. 'She thinks it is because of my illness that I can't choose right from wrong … boy from girl.'

'Who is Vatsala aunty to decide what's right for us and what's not?' Mehr turned Anahita towards her.

'She is my mother, Mehr. She loves me. Even when my father gave up on me after that stabbing incident in school, she did not. She went through every pain because of me, for me. She ensured I received a normal teenager's life despite all the villainy that surrounded me after the incident. Even you were not there, Mehr.'

'I was not there because my parents took me away from you. They thought you were obsessed with me and that is why you stabbed that bastard.'

'And you did not choose to stay back for me, did you?' Anahita's voice was accusing.

'I was only fourteen back then. But now we are adults! We can't let them decide for us. I know you cannot love anybody else … just like me.' Tears danced in her eyes, even as she tried to hold them back.

'When you knew I had feelings for you, why did you even go out with that bastard?'

'Because I didn't know back then, Anu. Can you really say you did? We were conditioned like that.'

'I love you, Mehr,' Anahita whispered through tears. 'I will always love you. But I can't do this. I have to go back. I can't be in touch with you. I am sorry.'

'I can't stop you if that's your decision. And you may move on, but if you ever need me … just call. I will always be there for you.'

'I wish I could just close my eyes, and when I open them, I could see you wherever I am, whenever I want.'

'I love you, Anu.' Mehr kissed Anahita on the lips. It was the first time … and the last.

59

Present Day
7E, Paradise Heights

WHEN ANAHITA WOKE UP, THE FIRST THING SHE SAW was Mehr sitting beside her on the bed. That proximity reminded Anahita of the kiss that happened nine years ago – the kiss that symbolized Anahita's ultimate sacrifice. It dented Anahita's urge for being loved. The kiss that paved the way for Varun in her life. The longing for that kiss had brought her back to Mumbai. That haunting kiss brought her back to that moment of chaos in her present.

'Where am I? What happened? Where is Varun?' Anahita asked. Scattered images flashed before her eyes – of fire engulfed in black smoke rising in the air.

'Relax, Anahita. Here' – Mehr picked up the bottle of water, poured some into a glass, and handed it to Anahita – 'have this first.'

Anahita sipped the water and asked, 'Was it … another dream?'

Mehr took a long breath. 'I wish. Keshav didn't survive. Varun has suffered major burns and is in the ICU.'

'I want to see him.' Anahita's eyes were brimming with tears.

'No. I won't let you leave this house. It is for your own good.' Mehr clutched Anahita's right hand and hugged her tightly.

'But this is all because of me,' Anahita cried. 'It is because of me.'

'No, it is because of that bastard, Deshmukh. He is the real villain of this story. And I will make sure that I expose him before he gets to any of us. But first, I need to get you out of here. You need to be safe. I know him well and he must have already planted the seeds to get you into trouble.'

Before Anahita could say anything, the doorbell rang.

60

As Bhau had instructed, Godbole and his deputy showed up to take Anahita in custody. The idea was to divert the media's attention to the woman and deem her as a psychotic serial killer. There were a dozen channels in Hindi, English and Marathi, that were waiting for a sensational media trial.

When the two officers arrived at the door, Mehr could smell the fishy fumes of conspiracy. She was prepared to handle the commissioner at their door.

Godbole stood at the door and asked, 'What is your connection with Ferozie Irani?'

'I have already told you, we will not answer any of your questions in this manner. You don't have official orders to interrogate Anahita.'

'We are doing our duty, Ms Hussain.'

'We went to see him as part of an investigation I was doing for a story. That's all.'

'And what about Hira Tejwani? Did Ms Anahita Anand visit him for the same purpose?'

The name took Mehr and Anahita by surprise. 'What about Tejwani? How is he involved in this?'

'Well, Tejwani's body was found today in his apartment. His head was also decapitated in the same way as Ferozie's. We think it might be the work of the same person – a serial killer.'

'And on what basis are you questioning us?'

'Stop acting like a lawyer from a Hollywood film, Ms Hussain. We have an eyewitness who places you and your friend at the victim's place – the scene of crime – the day Ferozie was murdered. He has also seen Mrs Anahita Anand with the man called Hira Tejwani.'

'Eyewitness?' Mehr and Anahita exchanged confused looks.

'Yes. But, of course, he's dead now. As part of the car explosion. Conveniently, the two of you were out of the car when the accident happened.'

'Keshav?' Anahita asked in disbelief.

'Yes, Keshav. He had given a video statement earlier in the day. We are also investigating into what caused the accident that killed Keshav.'

'Look, Godbole,' Mehr spoke up before Anahita could say anything to unwittingly implicate herself, 'my friend is unwell. She also witnessed a traumatic accident involving her husband.' Mehr tried to suppress her anger and spoke gently. 'I will request you to go away now. You can talk to her psychiatrist.'

'Dr Shetty has already given her statement that, seemingly, Mrs Anand's condition has deteriorated rapidly. But the doctor suspects that her apparent mental illness could be a sham to hide her crimes.' Godbole looked over Mehr's shoulder at Anahita, who crashed on the sofa behind her. 'It is true, isn't it, Mrs Anand?'

'This is no way to talk to her. I know how law deals with suspects. I must ask you to go or I will expose the nexus that is behind all this,' Mehr warned. 'I know you work for Bhau and that accident was also planned by him.'

'Ms Hussain, there are a lot of pending cases that involve crashed choppers and cars hit by trucks in Indian courts. The cases go on forever.' Godbole adjusted his cap. 'Right now, I am asking with a lot of patience and restrictions. If you don't cooperate, I will return with an arrest warrant for Mrs Anand.'

'That would be better. Don't make me turn on my camera and go live with this unofficial interrogation, Godbole.' Mehr pulled out her phone and waved it.

Godbole retreated. 'You think this is over? I will be back soon with an arrest warrant.'

'Goodbye!' Mehr said furiously and slammed the door on his face. She walked hurriedly towards Anahita, who was sobbing. 'No, no … don't be afraid. You have to be strong now. This is going to get shittier.'

'I don't even know what is happening. How did those people die? Ferozie and Tejwani!'

'I can guess how they died. Keshav was Bhau's handy man – a mercenary. He killed them on Bhau's orders, and then Bhau planned to erase all of us together with that accident. But that plan didn't work. We are alive, and we are alive for a reason, I believe. Anahita, you are the reason we got out of that cab. We are alive, Anahita, because this is your destiny. Maybe this is all happening because it is your destiny to expose that corrupt bastard.'

Anahita looked into Mehr's eyes, trying to find meaning in what she claimed, 'What?'

'You coming to Mumbai, moving into this house, your hallucinations about Parizaad, your encounter with me – it was all leading to the same destination through a common destiny. Anu, you believed that Parizaad's ghost was telling you something. You convinced me to help you, and we found Bhau's connection to the dead woman. We have rocked his world with these revelations that were buried twenty years ago. If I go with your word that Parizaad's ghost visited you, then she wanted to expose Bhau for some reason. We have to find out what that is.'

Anahita did not speak. She sniffled a little, but the crying subsided. Instead of breaking down, Mehr was all pumped-up.

'Bhau is powerful. He has already got you trapped as a serial-killer suspect. I am equally trapped as your accomplice. As far as I know him, he will get authorities to hold me responsible for the car accident as well. Anahita, we have very little time. We must act now.'

'How? Anahita said finally.

'I am going live on Facebook with you.'

61

'MOST OF YOU MUST HAVE SEEN ME IN THE NEWS, AT least those who regularly watch English news channels. I am Mehrab Hussain, a journalist and the founder-editor of *The Indie*. I've always believed that unmasking the rogues of our society is my job. I started by exposing some famous television actors with my sting operations. I occasionally appear on news debates as well.' She cleared her voice. 'In a few hours from now, India's most watched English news channel, which is involved in a TRP scam, will broadcast a well-scripted interview with Dayanand Deshmukh, the man you all know as Bhau.' Mehr spoke boldly looking into her phone's camera. There were distortions in the video broadcast because of the bad network in Anahita's study.

'This man, Bhau, that we know as great and revolutionary has hidden a dark past. When my friend and I came closer to digging up the buried past, he played an extremely wicked game against us. You must have already heard rumours of a serial killing streak in the city. If not, then you will hear about it tomorrow, because tonight, the news channels will completely focus on Bhau's big interview. So, wait for it. But

237

guess what guys, I am going to introduce you to the serial killer. She is here with me. You'll see her first on my Facebook live.' Mehr panned the camera and brought Anahita into focus. 'There, see? This is my friend, Anahita. Bhau and his powerful loyalists in the police have planted evidence that points at her. Within twenty-four hours, Bhau's ass-licking commissioner will arrest my friend for the murders. Tell me guys, does she look like a serial killer?' Mehr paused for a moment as she noticed the number of viewers crossing four digits. Mehr focused the camera back on herself and continued, 'Bhau, I know you will see this soon and you will try to speed up your plans. You tried to finish us all by hitting our car with a truck. You killed your own hitman, Keshav, because you did not need him anymore. But you got him to record a testimony stating that he had taken Anahita to Ferozie and Hira's places. Very smart! Bhau, you've almost killed Anahita's spouse, who was also working to project your nephew as the next CM candidate for Maharashtra. You may kill me and Anahita too, but you cannot kill our spirits that will live on in the minds of those people who will watch this video. The spirit of Anahita will torment the tyrant.'

Mehr took a deep breath and continued, 'We'll question you, Bhau. No matter how. You can eliminate us or vindicate us in false cases, but you cannot shut us up. You may buy off a few greedy jokers, but there are journalists who still abide by the ethics, who will fight this battle even if you finish us. Our spirits will live on in the minds of such people, just like the spirit of Parizaad has lived on in the mind of my friend, Anahita. So, beware Mr Dayanand Deshmukh. The world will know Parizaad's truth. You *will* be answerable.'

The broadcast ended. Mehr looked at Anahita. 'That was a digital suicide note,' she said and forced a smile.

'Now what?' Anahita asked.

'Now, we wait.'

Minutes later, Mehr's phone rang. The name of the caller appeared on the screen. She expected calls from many people, but that person was not in her list of expected callers. Mehr answered.

'Mehrab *beta*, I am sorry about how things are right now … ' It was the quivering voice of an aged man, interrupted by coughs. 'I am extremely unwell, but please come see me. I think I have the missing link you are looking for.'

'On my way,' Mehr said and disconnected the phone. She requested Anahita to lock the door and not to allow anyone inside until she returned.

62

Bhau's study room

'THAT FUCKING VIDEO IS VIRAL! EVERYONE HAS SEEN IT,' Bhau shouted. 'I am getting calls. Some people from the opposition have gheraoed my nephew's *dharna*,' he said as he sat on his leather recliner.

'You underestimated the power of that woman and her journalist friend,' the scavenger said, dropping two cubes of ice in his drink.

'How would I know that the woman would get out at that moment? Fortune favoured her,' Bhau said, his eyes following the movement of the scavenger across the room. The lean man in the black suit finally settled on a sofa.

'You should have killed her as soon as you got suspicious. This video should not have happened. Both of us have a lot to lose if they uncover anything more.'

'What do we do now?' Bhau looked at the scavenger in desperation. He hoped that the devious mind had the solution, as always.

The scavenger swirled his glass. The ice cubes inside started melting into the alcohol, 'Ice cubes melt faster in alcohol when we swirl them like this. But be careful because if you move even a bit faster, the alcohol can spill on your clothes.'

'What?'

'It is time for you to finish this. You take care of the husband and the journalist. I'll handle the mad woman. We do it like we did it twenty years ago. But do it gently so that it doesn't spill on you.'

63

SOMEWHERE INSIDE A SHABBY OLD SHANTY IN WORLI, Mehr eagerly searched for a folder inside a rusted almirah. She finally got hold of one that read *Parizaad & the Vultures*. Mehr pulled out the green folder and brought it to the frail man lying on the bed made of corroding wrought iron.

'You had this with you all this time, Amol ji?' Mehr asked, handing it over.

Amol Abhyankar let out a small laugh and said, 'I had come to you with whatever I had few weeks ago. You said nobody is interested in stale stories, remember, beta?'

Mehr sighed, realizing that the veteran journalist was absolutely correct.

Amol said, 'This story was one of those.'

Mehr felt sorry for having dismissed his wish. He looked pale and bonier than ever. She knew something was wrong with him. 'I am sorry for not considering any of your stories that day.'

'That is okay, beta. I like your style of reporting. You remind me of myself back in the day; you know, before all that happened. I also tried to expose that bastard in 1999. He trapped me and tainted me forever. Now, I see he has done the same to you and your friend,' Amol said with a glimmer of hope that simmered in his cataract-ridden eyes. 'He won't back off from taking your lives, because he did not even spare his lover when she posed a threat to him.'

'Lover?' Mehr asked, surprised at the choice of words.

'The woman whom you have been tracking, Parizaad, was Bhau's lover.'

'Right, that is why he had signed on her consent form,' Mehr said. 'I suspected that too, but I don't have enough evidence except for a consent form from the hospital where she gave birth to their child. Any guardian can sign consent forms. But why would Bhau kill her? Did he kill the daughter too?'

'I assume so. Parizaad was trying to solve the mystery of the disappearing vultures in the region. She sought my help. We became good friends. Our investigation led us to a similar scenario that happened in South Africa roughly during the same time. Vultures died in large numbers. The researchers found traces of a drug called diclofenac in their stomachs. These came from the dead remains of cattle that those vultures consumed. Farmers administered diclofenac to cattle to ease pain and inflammations. We also sent samples of dead vulture specimen from the local areas and found traces of diclofenac in their bodies. This led us to interrogate farmers who revealed that the agriculture ministry had supplied large quantities of a Russian drug at subsidized rates. Bhau, the agriculture minister back then, had made the deal with the Russian company for an enormous sum of money. They imposed the new drug on farmers in place of the safer ones, and they believed it would work as the agricultural ministry claimed. Those in power can convince the poor and illiterate farmers, just like they do not allow mating of cows in some places stating that it might produce unhealthy offspring. The poor farmers believe the authority and accept genetically modified semen provided to them. Bhau made a fortune and some powerful friends who promised more funds, which he used to grow his influence over powerful people. He bought more people on his side and suppressed anyone who spoke against him. Bhau maintained a clean image. His dirty transactions were carried out by this friend who had put him in touch with the Russian drug company. In fact, the friend co-owned the company. When the drug was banned in Moscow, the Russian partners put the onus on the Indian partner to sell off the stocks. Parizaad had tracked down this friend and was about to reveal the entire game to the world, but then they got to her first.'

'Who is this friend? Did she tell you?' Mehr asked impatiently.

'She called him *the scavenger*. I know nothing else because she was going to reveal everything through an article that she was writing for the next day's newspaper. She died before she could complete it. They killed her. They killed the daughter too, I guess. They already knew that her family thought she was mad. So, they used their friends in the crime branch to make it appear as a suicide committed by a mad woman after she performed a cannibalistic human sacrifice of her daughter. They tainted her and erased her from the pages of the past, so that nobody ever talked about her.'

'And now they are doing the same with Anahita.'

'Yes, these documents have enough proof to bring the truth out in the open for the vultures in the media to scavenge.'

'Why didn't you expose them earlier?'

'How do you think I ended up in jail? They filed a fake case against me and put me behind bars. The goons tortured me in jail. By the time I came out, nobody wanted me near them. Nobody was ready to hire me. I tried to give this report to a big newspaper back in 2012, but the editor burnt it to ashes in front of me. Bhau became the chief minister. He was funding almost every major corporate media house in the region. The poor journalists could do nothing. The corporate houses tried to destroy anything that could harm Bhau's image as long as he was funding them through advertisements or otherwise. Of course, the loyalty keeps changing as the donor changes. So many journalists are tainted because of some destructive elements in the fraternity. When Bhau lost in 2015, I tried again, but he still was able to pull a few strings. Eventually, I gave up. I thought of ending this life of starvation. But I hung on to these stories. Although I stopped believing in it, but I guess it was destiny that kept me alive for such a long time. Any day now, I can die, such is my condition. I am glad you made this video before I died. Else, I would have not been able to help you, your friend … ' Amol took a deep breath, 'and Parizaad.'

'Do you have any idea who this friend of Bhau is?' Mehr asked.

'I don't know. He has connections with people high up the ladder in every department. There are rich, influential people from the film fraternity backing Bhau. Police officers, diplomats, media persons, superstar actors; it could be anyone.

Bhau has powerful loyalists. Besides, it is all about favours with those in power.'

Mehr first thought about Godbole, who had come barging into Anahita's apartment a few hours back, and then she thought of the film personalities who had sided with Bhau.

'I think I know who it might be,' she said. 'Thank you, Amol ji. You have always been an inspiration. I will make sure that your efforts and pain do not go in vain.'

'Now, do the right thing, beta.'

64

———

ANAHITA LOCKED HERSELF INSIDE THE BEDROOM. EVERY passing second felt like a dagger waiting to stab her. Her heartbeats were faster than ever; the scenes of the car going up in flames did not leave her mind.

'Why? Why did you do this to me? What wrong did I do to deserve this?' She yelled. 'Where the hell have you disappeared? Why aren't you haunting me anymore? You must be laughing somewhere looking at my diabolical fate.'

Anahita cried out desperately hoping for a sign from the ghost of the dead woman or the vulture. Nothing happened.

'I shouldn't have believed you. I should have listened to my husband and the doctor.'

As a thunder gurgled outside, a crack appeared on the wall of the room, and it started shaking. The surrounding walls started moving inwards – another hallucination triggered by the panic attack.

Anahita closed her eyes tightly.

Breathe in. Breathe out.

She focused on the sound of her deep breaths. The sound of rain remained constant in the background. Her heart continued to pound and everything else fell silent.

Everything is not under our control.

In that silence, she heard metal clinking inside the keyhole of the main door. The front door opened, and she heard footsteps approaching the room. In the silence, she heard a hand turning the knob of the door to her bedroom. The door creaked as it opened along with Anahita's eyes as she looked at the man standing at the door. He had a gun pointed at Anahita. She did not recognize him.

It was the scavenger.

65

ALL THE WATERLOGGING FROM THE CONTINUOUS rainfall had resulted in heavy traffic congestions. Mehr boarded a cab from Amol Abhyankar's place in Worli. The cab was stuck somewhere on Jagmohan Das Marg. She went through the files that Amol had given her while in the cab. There were many reports as Amol had mentioned – medical studies, transaction details, bank account details, newspaper cuttings. There were also photographs, old film camera ones, of himself, Parizaad and some of their activist friends. She wondered what those candid photographs were doing in that folder. *Maybe Amol buried the effigies of Parizaad here.* However, one photo grabbed her eyeballs.

It was a picture of Parizaad candidly playing with a young girl, about seven years old – her daughter. Mehr had seen the girl in the photograph before – long ago, but not so long ago.

66

～

I NSIDE HER ROOM, ANAHITA LOOKED ON, FROZEN IN FEAR. The scavenger's face wasn't clear in the dark.

'Bhau liked Varun, you know, he had a bright future. He would have made a great team with Abhinav, but I had to do it. It is not my fault though; it is yours. You should have kept yourself away from all of this,' the scavenger said coldly.

The scavenger gazed at the walls. Anahita watched him helplessly.

'This house has lots of memories,' he said. 'Bhau did not want anyone else to experience those memories. Memories of Parizaad … She should have waited, but she threatened to destroy my identity. Do you know how difficult it is to build one in this selfish little world of ours?' The scavenger aimed the semi-automatic at Anahita's chest. 'And after all these years, you ruined it for us. You—'

The scavenger's voice was disrupted by the sound of Anahita's phone ringing – a call from Mehr's number. He pulled the trigger, and a bullet fired out of the handgun's muzzle.

The bullet missed Anahita by inches and hit the wall behind her. In shock, Anahita scrambled and fell off the bed, her hand smashing the framed photo collage on the bedside table. It landed near the scavenger's feet. The glass broke and a crack formed over the photo collage. As he looked down, his eyes fell on one particular photo in the collage. It was of a beautiful young girl; a girl whose face he could not forget.

'How? What is this girl's photo doing here? He had them removed … then …' Realization dawned upon the scavenger.

Anahita, still trying to absorb the scary turn of events, looked at the broken photo frame and then at the dumbstruck scavenger. He was saying something, but she was too shocked to process it.

Something inside Anahita's head shouted – *RUN!*

67

Five minutes ago

'HELLO, VATSALA AUNTY. THIS IS MEHR.'

'Mehr?' A woman's thick voice responded, displeased at hearing the girl's voice.

'Yes, aunty.'

'What do you want?'

'I want the truth. Who is Anahita?'

'What?' Vatsala barked. 'We are already going through a lot of trouble. You have always been a bad influence on her. You have proved it once again …'

'Aunty, I would like to know the truth, please. It would be better if you tell me now or else, I might be forced to tell the police that you kidnapped a girl twenty years ago.' Mehr stared at the photograph of the young girl with Parizaad. 'I have proof.'

Silence from the other side.

'I don't have a lot of time. Neither does Anu. So …' Mehr pressed.

'What do you mean? Is she …'

'The truth can help her. Vatsala aunty, are you Anu's real mother?'

'No!' Vatsala paused. 'She came in front of our car while we were in Mumbai. I was driving. I didn't see the girl because of the rain. I had caused the accident that wiped out Anahita's memory. All she remembered was her name. I had informed the police, but no one came to claim her. It was like she didn't have anyone at all.' Vatsala wept. 'I could never have a child. I decided to keep her even though my husband was against it. We never told her that she belonged to someone else. Yes, Mehr, Anahita is not my biological daughter.'

'Thanks aunty.' Mehr paused and let the information sink. 'Vatsala aunty … you have been a great support to Anu … a great mother.' Mehr heard the woman on the other side let out a soft cry.

'Is she okay?'

'She will be. Bye.'

Mehr disconnected the call, and dialled another number. The phone was not answered. She dialled again and this time it was answered by Bhau.

'I know you think that you have cornered us.' Mehr waited for a response but there wasn't any. 'But I have something that will make you repent everything that you have planned with the scavenger,' Mehr said sharply into the phone.

'What scavenger?'

'Bhau. I know about your daughter.'

'What the hell are you talking about?' Bhau was disturbed.

'The scavenger lied to you. Your daughter is alive and I know where she is right now.'

Silence from the other end.

Mehr asked, 'Don't you want to see your daughter?'

68

17 August 2019, Saturday
7E, Paradise Heights, Mumbai

ANAHITA COULD NOT RUN OUT OF THE ROOM BECAUSE the scavenger stood in the way. She ran towards the glass door, opened it, and jumped onto the balcony. A part of the curtain clung to her dress and got stuck in the door's roller, as Anahita stood outside, getting drenched in the rain.

The scavenger stood on the other side of the glass; his soulless eyes locked on to Anahita's horror-stricken face. Anahita could see the scavenger clearly now. She remembered those eyes. Though they had aged, they kept the same characteristic soullessness. A feeling of Déjà vu crept in. This had happened before, twenty years ago …

19 July, twenty years ago

'Mom?' seven-year-old Anahita woke from her dreams. 'Why are you crying, mom?'

Parizaad gathered all the courage that she could. 'Promise me you will be a brave girl tonight?'

Little Anahita nodded.

'Then come with me.'

Little Anahita got up from the bed and held on to her mother's right hand. Together, they walked out to the open balcony. High above the ground, the skies seemed closer. Thunder gurgled, sending bolts of lightning into the night sky. Dark clouds had gathered over them.

Meanwhile, the scavenger had slid open the glass door after tearing off the freshly written page from Parizaad's diary. She saw him staring right into her soul. She clenched her fingers around her daughter's wrist, trying to hide the girl behind her back. There was nothing else she could do at this point. Little Anahita, hiding behind her mother, turned her head to look beyond the parapet – *vertigo*! The girl closed her eyes, clenching on to her mother's back.

The scavenger tilted his head diabolically, aimed the gun at Parizaad's head, and delivered a lethal headshot. Little Anahita opened her eyes at the sound and saw blood splattering from her mother's head. She shrieked in horror, but the scavenger's hand was on her mouth so that her sound could not escape. She bit him and ran inside. He followed. She was about to lock it, but the scavenger had already put his leg inside. She slid the door shut. He let out a cry, but slid open the door and furiously entered the bedroom. He grabbed her by the tip of her ponytail and slammed her on the corner wall. The impact hurt her right shoulder badly as she fell on the floor. She was trapped and at his mercy. She had promised to be a brave girl that night. Amidst tears, she gathered all the strength she could and rose on her feet. She ran out of the bedroom and then out of the house.

Minutes later, she was out of the apartment. Little Anahita ran in the rain, passing by the back gate. She ran as far as she could. As she scurried on the road, a car hit her. Everything that had happened faded into the background as her head hit the road. Anahita lost consciousness, her mother's voice ringing in her ears: 'I love you. I will always be here for you, Anahita.'

⁓

Present Day

The *tabula* or slate wasn't blank anymore because Anahita remembered things that happened on that fateful day in 1999. She remembered the soulless eyes of the scavenger. She remembered that the woman in the maroon dress who was shot dead was her biological mother – Parizaad. She remembered the things that happened moments before the car accident, which wiped out her memories. The erased prologue from Anahita's life found a way of crawling back when history repeated itself twenty years later.

Anahita was at the edge of the balcony, her hand on the parapet's railing. She looked down; the scene gave her vertigo just like it had twenty years ago. Far away, the green patch of land, the dakhma, seemed to call. She took a couple of deep breaths and turned. The scavenger was standing right there, like a predator eyeing its prey. He held the picture of little Anahita which he tore from the photo collage.

'I could never forget that seven-year-old girl's face.' The scavenger crumpled the picture. 'It was you!' He started inching towards Anahita. 'That day you escaped. However, I had found you again when that woman who had rammed her car into you informed the police. But then I came to know that you had lost your memory, and I thought … what harm can a girl with no memory do to us?' The scavenger grabbed Anahita by the wrist. 'I underestimated you that day … never again.'

'Why?' Anahita said, tears streaming down her eyes. 'Why did you kill my mother?'

'I had to protect some secrets – *your* father's secrets … ' He lifted the handgun and placed it on Anahita's forehead. 'I hope you know by now who he is.'

Anahita had also connected the dots – Parizaad's lover was Dayanand Deshmukh, therefore he was Anahita's biological father. Bhau was her father.

The scavenger laughed. 'Ooh. By the way, you have your mother's voice.' He didn't realize that a dark shadow was hovering behind him.

Anahita's back touched the railings. Right in front of her stood the scavenger, with a gun pointed at her forehead. She did not have any escape route. This was it. This was how he had killed her mother twenty years ago. This was how it felt … the last moments before death.

'Did you know the day I killed Parizaad was also a Saturday?' The scavenger winked as he placed his finger on the trigger.

'Yes, I do,' said a ghastly voice that didn't tremble at all. It came from behind. The scavenger turned around. At the glass door stood a woman in a maroon dress, her eyes raging with fury. The fact that the scavenger had murdered that very woman twenty years ago sent a shiver down his spine.

69

⁓

THE CAB STOPPED IN FRONT OF THE APARTMENT'S GATE. Mehr threw a five hundred rupee note at the driver and rushed to the gate. She hid Amol's folder under her shirt to protect it from the rain. The watchman was repairing the CCTV camera. Mehr was sprinting towards the entrance of Anahita's building when something heavy dropped behind her with a thud.

Mehr stopped and turned around. Other residents came out into their balconies at the sound. All eyes were stuck to the same spot on the ground – sprawled on the concrete floor, a body, blood pooling under it, merging with the raindrops. Mehr looked at the face of the person in shock. She knew the person well. He was the funder of *The Indie* and one of Bhau's all-weather friends: Ashwath Daevendra Desai.

But what is Desai doing here?

At that moment, Mehr realized a shocking truth. Bhau's partner-in-crime that Amol Abhyankar tried to track was Desai. The man who killed Parizaad twenty years ago was Desai.

As she stood there in the rain, looking at the lifeless body of Desai, Mehr remembered what Nariman had said about the yazata – *Whenever there is injustice, like the splashing waters of a violent rain, she'll torment the tyrant daevas and bring them to justice.*

Ashwath Daevendra Desai was the scavenger.

'Please call the police. Now!' Mehr instructed the guard who had come running. She rushed towards the elevator.

A few minutes later, Mehr was on the seventh floor. The door to 7E was ajar. She went inside, calling out to her friend, 'Anu?' No reply. Mehr's heart thumped in suspense, fearing the worst. When she walked past the living room, and into the bedroom, she could see the glass door was open and Anahita was lying flat on the balcony, drenched in the rain. Mehr dropped the file on the floor and ran to her friend.

'Anu … dear … You are alive … what just happened here? How did you …' Mehr helped Anahita get up. 'Did you push him down?'

'No, I didn't.' Anahita steadied herself with difficulty. 'If I tell you what happened, will you believe me or call it another one of my hallucinations?'

'I will believe every word you say,' Mehr said, 'because I just had the greatest shock of my life. Tell me.'

'*She* saved me,' Anahita muttered, tears cascading down her cheeks.

'Who?'

'The woman at the glass door. She came. She pushed him and then *flew* away.'

'What woman?'

'Parizaad. My Mother. *She* was my vulture.'

Mehr wanted to tell Anahita that it had to be a hallucination. Dead people do not come back from their graves. Mehr deduced Anahita must have subconsciously pushed Desai off the roof, or he must have tripped on the wet floor and fallen. Besides, there were no vultures in the region. Vultures were almost extinct in Mumbai.

Anahita knew exactly what Mehr was thinking. She smiled and pointed towards the sky. Mehr looked up in the direction. Fluttering its wings mightily against the tyrant rain was a long-billed gypsy vulture. It soared up in the sky and glided towards the green patch of land in the heart of the bustling city – *the dakhma.*

Every strand of hair on Mehr's body stood on end.

Tears filled up Mehr's eyes as she saw the bird disappear in the distance. 'You had always been right, Anu.' Mehr turned and looked at Anahita. 'It was indeed your destiny.'

'Our destiny,' Anahita said, leaning in for a kiss in the rain.

Epilogue

Eighteen months later
Mehr's Residence, Mumbai

IT WAS A BEAUTIFUL MORNING IN MUMBAI, AND THE SUN was shining warmly. The city administration had recently lifted its lockdown restrictions, and people had started visiting friends and relatives again. An airport cab was parked outside Mehr's apartment.

Inside, Dr Malhotra was having a hot cup of tea and warm pakoras, with Anahita and Mehr. Their masks resting peacefully on the dining table.

'You look chubbier than the last time I saw you, Anahita. Seems like Mumbai's air has worked for you.' The psychiatrist flashed a sweet smile.

'Honestly, the credit goes to Mehr. If it wasn't for her, I would not have survived, especially after Varun's death.'

'Oh please, Anu,' Mehr cut in. 'You are the reason *I* survived. If it wasn't for your die-hard spirit and belief, neither of us would have survived that scavenger Desai's trap.'

'I am sorry, Anahita. Instead of believing you, I thought you had lost your mind completely,' Dr Malhotra said. 'It is just incredible how the truth came out. The two of you exposed one of the biggest cover ups in India.'

'I don't blame you. No sane person would ever believe *what* led us to the truth,' Anahita said, thinking of the vulture that disappeared into the dakhma. She added with a calm smile on her face, 'It was destiny.'

A baby cooed from the master bedroom. Anahita instinctively got up to check on the baby. Mehr stopped her. 'I will check on baby Parizaad.' Mehr left the room, leaving a much calmer Anahita with her former psychiatrist.

'It's sweet that you named your girl after your *real* mother,' Dr Malhotra said. 'I hope Vatsala is okay with all of this.'

'She *is* and *will* be my mother. She raised me. She had been carrying the guilt of causing the accident, and the burden of hiding the truth about my biological mother. But like I said, it was all destined. If that accident had not happened, then that scavenger Desai would have killed me in 1999. Nobody would have unearthed Bhau's rotten scandal, and Parizaad wouldn't have had justice!'

'Yeah, life works in weird ways, Anu. I saw it on TV, how Bhau confessed to all his crimes on a live news broadcast. He looked defeated, burdened by guilt. I could see from his eyes. It took his own daughter to bring down the tyrant.'

'Daughter? No.' Anahita shook her head. Her eyes were stone cold. 'I couldn't accept Bhau as my father. Didn't feel the connect or the need for such a man who was so bothered about his public perception and personal goals that he ordered for the execution of his ex-lover and child.' The words came out strongly, unusual for Anahita. She added, 'His apology or repentance means nothing to me.'

'I am sorry if I said too much there.'

'No. Not really.' Anahita smiled. She changed the topic. 'Doc, what's with the dark circles? Aren't you sleeping well?'

Dr Malhotra shifted in the chair. 'Actually, something happened that's been keeping me up. In fact, I wasn't feeling safe in Gurugram anymore. So, I came here to my son's place in Malad. But more importantly, I had to warn you.'

Noticing the shift in the psychiatrist's voice, Anahita asked, 'Warn me? About what?'

'This is related to that stabbing incident which happened when you were in school. Did you hear anything about that boy, Christopher, after that?'

The calmness on Anahita's face started fading away as she thought about one of her former nightmares. 'I heard he had complications, but survived. I changed my school, so I know nothing more.'

'He survived all right, but the trauma took a toll on his mental health, which was made worse by his abusive step mother. In 2007, he attempted to kill his step mother. After that they kept him in a mental correctional facility. He was there for a very long time … tortured and tormented in the name of treatment.' Dr Malhotra's voice trailed off.

A moment of uncomfortable silence.

'What is it, doctor?' Beads of sweat formed on Anahita's forehead. 'Tell me!'

'For the last few days, I have felt like I am being stalked. During morning walks, and at night while walking back to my house from MG Road station. And then it happened –

two nights ago, while walking home from the metro station, a man intercepted me,' the psychiatrist said in a shaky voice. 'Strangely, he was asking for you. He told me his name was Christopher. His face was not visible clearly in the darkness, but his left eye looked disfigured. When he saw a couple of police officers patrolling, he slipped away into the night. After coming home, I remembered the boy you stabbed in school. You had poked a compass into his left eye. So, I called up the mental correctional facility.'

'Did he escape the correctional facility?' Anahita asked, alarmed, her fingers fidgeting.

'Worse.' Dr Malhotra held Anahita's hands. She tried to keep her hand steady, but with fear-filled eyes, she said, 'Christopher died in a fire that broke out at the mental hospital, *two months* ago.'

Acknowledgements

First, thanks to you for choosing this book to read. The idea for this book came before the pandemic and the first draft happened during the lockdown. Grateful to corona warriors all over the world for their thankless service to humankind.

Thanks to my teachers and administration at DAVPS (Sector 14) Gurugram for being so supportive in my journey as a storyteller.

I am grateful to Cyrus Mistry's *Chronicle of a Corpse Bearer* – a book that moved me deeply. Thankful to the lectures of Paul Bloom and the books on psychology that I referred before writing – *Phantoms in the Brain: Probing the Mysteries of the Human Mind* by Sandra Blakeslee and V. S. Ramachandran, and *Psychology* by Saundra K. Ciccarelli, J. Noland White and Girishwar Misra.

I'd like to thank the wonderful folks at HarperCollins India for making India's Most Haunted so memorable for me – Diya Kar, Arcopol Chaudhry, Prateek, Mohan Raj, Sai Deverekonda and team. Thanks to Ateendriya Gupta for the valuable inputs. Extending my gratitude to my publisher – Udayan Mitra.

I am extremely grateful to the three most important people without whom this book wouldn't have been possible – Lakshmi, my mother, who believed in my passion. Pooja, my spouse, who has continued to believe in my dreams. And Prerna, the commissioning editor at HarperCollins India, who believed in this story. Thank you (I know I don't say that a lot).

About the Author

Hari Kumar, a.k.a. 'Horror Kumar', is an Indian screenwriter and bestselling author of horror and psychological thriller books, including *India's Most Haunted*. Hari was the first Indian writer to be listed on Amazon.com's top 100 bestsellers in the horror category.

He was born in Cochin and brought up in Gurgaon. He currently resides in Pune with his wife.